LEGACY OF LIES

Lexa M. Mack

iUniverse®

LEGACY OF LIES

iUniverse books may be ordered through booksellers or by contacting:

iUniverse
1663 Liberty Drive
Bloomington, IN 47403
www.iuniverse.com
844-349-9409

ISBN: 978-1-6632-3585-5 (sc)
ISBN: 978-1-6632-3586-2 (hc)
ISBN: 978-1-6632-3587-9 (e)

Library of Congress Control Number: 2022902873

Print information available on the last page.

iUniverse rev. date: 02/28/2022

For Kitty, thanks for 50 years of faith and encouragement.

CONTENTS

PROLOGUE

Friday, July 2

Detective Bobby Burns' car crested the hill near Alamo Square, gliding past the Victorian homes known as the "painted ladies" on his right. In the next block a police cruiser with lights flashing was parked against traffic on the left.

Traffic Guy had staked a claim to the curb in front of the bank of condos and after Bobby parked behind the black-and-white, he was directed up the stairs to the young officer standing at the bottom of another flight of stairs leading to two mirror-image condo doors, one ajar.

"Officer Regan, I understand you were first on scene."

"Yes, sir. We got a call from that guy over there that the woman in the condo was injured or sick and lying on the floor inside. I forced open the door and found the body."

"Nobody has been inside since then?"

"No, sir."

Bobby extracted a card of nicotine gum from his jacket pocket and punched a piece through the foil. "Okay, I'll go in and take a look. I assume Crime Scene and the coroner are on their way."

Again, "Yes, sir." From the look on the young officer's face, Bobby thought this might be Regan's first body. Always a milestone.

Before checking out the scene he went to speak with the distraught man sitting on the steps to the street. "I'm Detective Burns. You're the person who discovered the body?"

The man popped to his feet like a jack-in-the-box. "Yes, I came to check on Grace and saw her in there. I called the police right away. I already told everything to the officer."

"Yes, I just wanted to ask you a couple of questions. First, can you confirm your name?"

"My name is Doug, Doug Willis. I can't really tell you much. I just came to see if she was all right … and she wasn't."

"Are you a friend of the victim?"

"Victim? You mean somebody did this?"

"We don't really know what happened here. But you came to check on her because you know her, right?"

"Yes, she's a good friend; we were in college together. We work in the same office. She didn't come to work today and when I called there was no answer. I tried several times and then when she didn't show up by lunchtime, I came over here to see what was going on. We were supposed to have lunch, like we always do on Friday. We were going to try out that new Asian fusion place on Clement…"

Bobby put his hand on the man's shoulder, mostly to stop the flood of words. "So, you came and knocked on the door and when nobody answered what did you do?"

Doug turned toward the building. "I climbed up on that stair railing to see if she was in there, and I saw her on the floor."

"Did you recognize her?"

"No, I couldn't see very well; the lights were off and I just assumed it was her."

"All right, then what did you do?"

"I called you, the police I mean. The officer over there came in a few minutes and he forced the door. We thought maybe she was just hurt and we didn't know who else would have a key."

The Crime Scene van pulled up on the street. "The officer has your contact information. You can leave. We will be in touch soon. You'll need to come to the station and sign a statement."

"Can't I wait until you find out what happened? It seems wrong to just leave her alone here."

"I know, but you aren't leaving her alone and we need to be able to do our job." Bobby paused. "We'll take good care of her. There's nothing you can do now."

"I guess I could go back to the office, but what would I tell everyone?" The man hesitated for a moment. "Maybe I'll just go home."

Doug glanced up toward the condo door once more and then, stuffing his hands in his pockets, he walked down the steps to Fulton Street.

Bobby pulled disposable gloves from his pocket and slipped them on as he ascended the stairs. The door on the right stood ajar and he carefully pushed it open. The unit was what realtors would call a one-plus bedroom: a step and a half up from a studio and a real bargain at half a million dollars in a city that favored the rich over the hardworking.

Standing in the door he surveyed the tidy living room, the tiny kitchen, and at the back, the bedroom. Small, but still better than his place.

A woman's body lay on the floor adjacent to the kitchen area.

It took just two minutes to complete a walk through the unit. Bed was made, clothes hung up. Two wine glasses and an unopened bottle of white wine sat on the coffee table. Condensation had pooled at the base of the bottle.

He paused at the row of framed pictures arranged on a bookshelf. A tingle of recognition ran down his spine, but then, these were familiar scenes: a group of laughing friends around a table, two smiling skiers posed at the top of a run, a family photo from a happier time. Maybe he had just done this kind of walk-through too many times.

No dishes in the sink, but when he lifted the lid of the garbage can the top item was the black plastic remains of a microwave container. No doubt the single fork was already in the dishwasher.

He flipped on the kitchen overhead light and squatted beside the body.

She lay on her back, her head turned at a sharp angle, and her hair swept across her face. A pool of congealed blood spread out beneath her head.

He carefully pushed back the swath of hair before his breath caught in his throat. Looking closer he reassured himself that this was not the woman he knew. Not her style, not her surroundings—not her. Still, he felt shaken.

The Crime Scene crew had entered the room with their equipment and air of efficiency. The condo felt even smaller than before. He left the crew to their work, pausing once more at the door to look back at the body.

Bobby stopped at the bottom of the steps and lit the cigarette he had bummed off one of the Crime Scene techs.

He'd done everything he could. Now they would wait for someone from the coroner's office to arrive.

At first look it could have been an accident, except that people who have accidents rarely get rid of their laptops and phones and turn off all the lights. He'd noted that her purse remained, and it didn't appear that anyone had ransacked the place, but still, who didn't have a phone or a laptop around? They'd check her car if she had one, and her office, but something felt off here.

A blue and white SUV marked SAN FRANCISCO MEDICAL EXAMINER pulled up behind the Crime Scene van double-parked on the street and Traffic Guy placed an orange cone behind it as Dr. Kirschman climbed out. She was a looker and single. He'd thought about asking her out a couple of times but there was just something strange about a woman who spent her day cheerfully dissecting bodies.

"Good morning, Detective Burns. How are you?" she chirped as she breezed past him up the stairs. Just weird.

He knew that she and Crime Scene would be checking not just the body, but the life of the person that lay there. Doors and drawers would be opened, calendars would be checked. They would keep an eye out for drugs and scraps of paper; whatever would help them know the woman a little better. Dr. Emma Kirschman and the SFPD were thorough and took their time.

The shadow Bobby stood in grew chill and he moved out to the sunny sidewalk keeping an eye out for the tech with the cigarettes. The nicotine patch beneath his shirt itched and he scratched it distractedly.

At the bottom of the long street the dome of San Francisco City Hall loomed. Just weeks before it had glowed with rainbow lights and teemed with Pride Day parade participants. Today it had returned to its stately gray self.

A loud horn blast and the screech of tires drew his attention just as an older woman darted across the street in his direction.

Nice, jaywalking right in front of the police. She was oblivious to everything but her target, which appeared to be him.

"Are you the officer in charge here?" She squinted at him through spiky eyelashes framed by thick glasses. She was nicely dressed and tiny. She tilted her head back to peer up at him.

"Yes, ma'am, I guess I am. Can I help you?" He figured she was annoyed by the all the disturbance in her lovely neighborhood.

"Yes, I want you to do something about people lurking around on my landing and unscrewing my porch light."

To Bobby this complaint ranked right up there with littering and people who didn't pick up their dog's droppings.

"Well, ma'am, I'm sorry that someone has been lurking around your house but we are here to investigate a possible crime."

She waved her hand at him dismissively. "I can see that, but you people didn't send anybody out when I called so I have to talk to you when I can."

The argument was valid; they probably hadn't responded to her complaints with what she would call due consideration, and here he was, a police officer, just standing around doing nothing.

"I'll tell you what, I have a few minutes. Why don't you give me your complaint and I will pass it on to the appropriate department?"

The shock of being taken seriously registered on her wrinkled but impeccably made-up visage before she grinned up at him. "You'll take down notes and everything?"

"Yes, ma'am." He pulled the black leather notebook and pen from his inside coat pocket.

Before he could change his mind a claw-like, beringed hand latched onto his lower arm and pulled him toward the street. He stopped for a moment and turned to one of the policemen who'd been observing their encounter. "Joe, I'll be across the street for a minute. Let me know when Dr. Kirschman is done."

He and the woman darted across the street and up the long flight of stairs to the landing. It was a remodeled Victorian perched on this steeply sloped street. As a result, the lower floor was one apartment and reaching the main floor required a significant climb. He was glad he didn't have to haul groceries up these steps.

"My apartment is here on the right, and Mr. Schlosser is on the left." She said no more about her neighbor but her tone was dismissive. Bobby figured they were not friends. "Last Wednesday night someone lurked out here on my landing for quite some time, and they unscrewed the porch light so nobody could see them."

"Did they knock or try to get into your apartment or were they trying to reach the upstairs tenants?"

The woman rolled her eyes at him. "No, this door in the middle is locked and leads up to the upstairs apartment. You ring the bell for them and they have to come down to let you in. Nobody knocked for Mr. Schlosser or me and nobody rang the bell for upstairs. They just stood out here for about half an hour and then they left. They didn't even have the decency to screw the light bulb back in."

"What did they do out here for half an hour?"

"Young man, I cannot see through doors and there is no window here, just the peephole. I could see that someone came up here, I could see that the light went out, and I could hear them clomp down the stairs when they left."

Bobby surveyed the street and noted that he could clearly see Dr. Kirschman kneeling next to the body in the apartment across the way. The drapes were fully open and the lights had been turned on to help their investigation. At night, with the lights on, there would have been a clear view.

"What did you do, Mrs. uh. . . I don't think you gave me your name."

"Natalie Woodstock, my name is Natalie Woodstock, and I called you, well not you, but I called the police. They just asked me if anyone was trying to get in and if it was an emergency and then told me someone would drive by." She clamped her lips shut disapprovingly, "But nobody ever came by and he left after a while."

"Are you sure it was a man? Has the person been back or has this ever happened before?"

Mrs. Woodstock hesitated for the first time. "No, I guess I don't know for sure it was a man, but I know I thought it was a man. It felt like a man. It never happened before, but I am going to get me a gun. I already asked my grandson to go to the gun store with me."

The idea of an armed Mrs. Woodstock the next time someone came up the stairs was not comforting.

"Is the porch light working now? Did you touch the bulb?"

"Yes, I had to drag a step-stool out here to reach it."

Bobby wrote down Mrs. Woodstock's story. "I am going to have an officer come over here and fingerprint the light fixture and bulb. I'm afraid they will have to take your fingerprints, as well. Do you know the woman who lived in that condo directly across the street?"

"I didn't know her. I knew of her; she never closed her drapes, so I probably knew more about her than I should have."

"Well, then, once I have a better idea what happened there, I may come back to talk to you."

The woman seemed delighted at the prospect and he left her soothed by his attentions and with the sound advice that getting a good security system was probably a better investment than a gun, no matter what a good deal her grandson had promised her.

As he left her door, he saw that Dr. Kirschman had packed up her bag and was descending the stairs, ready to speak with him. The dead wagon had added to the caravan parked on the street and two attendants waited at the bottom of the stairs to remove the corpse.

CHAPTER ONE

April 15

Grace's name suited her perfectly. She was blessed in so many ways: loving parents, a good education, a good job, a suitable (if sometimes disappointing) boyfriend, a dream condo in San Francisco. What was there to be unhappy about? Until recently, she hadn't been. Then her friend and co-worker, Doug Willis, found his birth father on Heritage.com. Sometime in their early friendship she had told Doug that she was adopted, and though Doug was raised by his mother, he did not know his father. Tenuous though that bond was, they had discussed it many times.

Since Grace was a little girl her parents had always told her she was adopted: specially chosen, their one and only child.

She'd lived in the right neighborhood, took the best vacations, hung out with the right crowd. All of this was something to be grateful for, right?

Then Doug had shown up at work one day, wearing a Cheshire Cat grin and dropping unsubtle hints about the results of his DNA test from Heritage. At first, she had been happy for him. He was a good friend and he was bubbling over with the excitement of having found his dad.

In the past they had talked about him being raised by a single mom and not having a father figure in his life. About halfway through the second bottle of wine he would tear up a bit about Cub Scout outings and fishing trips he'd missed out on. If she felt especially tipsy, she might chime in about wishing she knew about her real parents, although the comment was more a camaraderie thing than any actual curiosity on her part.

Doug's mom had not been much help in his search. She'd never told him who his father was, just that she and he had not been a good match, and she'd decided to have Doug on her own. He hadn't pressed her for information. It seemed ungrateful to insist on details; it was like telling his mom that she wasn't enough. The latest attempt had ended in tears, for both of them.

Then, one day, over lattes, he had confided to Grace that he had sent a saliva sample to Heritage, just to see if anything popped up. Grace was completely supportive. Poor Doug. It wasn't like he'd had doting adoptive parents like hers.

There was nothing really wrong with Doug's mom. From what Grace could tell, she'd been a pretty good parent, and Doug had not really missed out on anything, except maybe all those imaginary paternal bonding experiences that one sees in television commercials for high-end cars and Disney cruises. Still, it was better to know where you came from, wasn't it?

A few weeks later, he'd gotten the word. There was a real flesh- and-blood father out there. There was some excitement for a few days around waiting for email responses, then an incredible high over a planned dinner meeting, and just before the big night, a tearful, wine-soaked fear-fest at Grace's condo, most of which Grace couldn't remember, which was probably not a bad thing.

The morning after the big meet-up Grace had been intensely curious about what had happened, but Doug had played it cagey. First, he told her he couldn't tell her anything at the office, all the while making like he was bursting with things to tell. Then Doug insisted that going to lunch wouldn't provide adequate time to tell her everything. Finally, he'd offered to cook for her at his apartment and he would reveal all.

"Just break the date with Dick-head, he won't care." Grace's boyfriend, Kevin, was not Doug's favorite person.

If Kevin was surprised at having her change their plans, his response of "Sure babe, no problem, give me a call later in the week. Gotta go," didn't betray any hurt feelings.

Grace went to Doug's firmly determined to have no more than two glasses of wine. She wanted to be able to remember what was said. She brought the wine herself as she had experience with Doug's inability to choose good wine, suspecting that his criteria had more to do with price than quality.

Doug left the office early and went to great effort to reproduce the lavish dinner he'd shared with his dad the evening before. Grace doubted whether she would have wanted to eat the meal of duck breast on a bed of braised escarole accompanied by a parsnip purée and followed by Mexican chocolate lava cakes and crème anglaise on two successive nights if she were Doug. But it was a lovely dinner and paired nicely with the sparkling wine from the Napa Valley.

"Okay, Doug, no fooling now. I am stuffed with incredible food and a little tipsy, so there is nothing you can tell me that will be too much. What happened with your dad?"

"Okay, okay. The dinner was great. Kent, or Dad, was fine. Nice guy, successful, friendly, if a little surprised to have a grown son at this point in his life."

"So, why the big buildup? I was expecting some big deal with all the secrecy."

"Well, the surprise was that Kent brought his partner, Corey."

"Corey?"

"Yes, his partner, Corey. My dad is gay, and that's why he and Mom didn't work it out all those years ago."

Grace took a moment to stare at Doug, open-mouthed, and to reach out and grab the bottle to pour another glass of bubbly.

"Gay? Really? Wow…" It was difficult to decide what to say. "OMG, are you kidding?" didn't seem quite right. Neither did "How lovely for you." She decided to wait and see what came next from Doug.

"I know," he laughed. "What do you say to that? Problem is, the longer they talked about being together so long, about their fabulous life in the Castro for the past twenty-five years, and about their wonderful trips around the world, the more I wondered if I hadn't been raised by the wrong parent."

"You don't mean that."

"No, not really, but I couldn't help but wonder how things would have been if I'd been born twenty years later, when gay parents were more common."

The conversation wandered around and about and back again, resolving nothing, but also raising doubts in Grace's heretofore incurious mind. What really was the story about her being put up for adoption? Was she abused, abandoned, left in a basket on the church steps? Funny that she had never pursued the question. She didn't even know if her parents knew the whole story. She could ask them, she supposed, but couldn't imagine sitting in their sunny kitchen in Menlo Park and throwing the question out there over hot chocolate. Maybe she could bring it up at Easter dinner with her mother's two brothers, their families, and Dad's parents at the table. She thought not, though she imagined for a moment the stunned silence that would follow the enquiry. Did everyone know all the details except her? It made her uncomfortable even thinking about it, and Grace was not a person who liked discomfort.

At the end of the evening Grace decided that discretion was advised and left her car at Doug's, taking an Uber the few blocks to her condo on Fulton Street.

That discussion triggered Grace, for the first time, to wonder who her "real" parents were, and what the other possibilities for her life had been. Who had given her up, and why, and where were they now? She couldn't imagine a better life than she'd had, but why had her own family not wanted her?

She knew that there were adoption registries where birth parents and the children they gave up could connect if both parties consented. But, how awful would it be to register and discover that your birth parents had not come looking for you?

The next day she bought the Heritage kit. She'd find out if any relatives were lingering out there, hoping to connect with her, without really putting her self-esteem on the line. After all, nobody would know she'd even done it and if there wasn't anyone, she could just forget the whole thing. She didn't even have to send for the kit in the mail; she had seen them on the shelf at the local drugstore, between the in-home pregnancy tests and food allergy kits.

Buying the DNA sample kit and spitting in the little vial was a no-brainer. The hard part was waiting for the results. The website had promised results in four to six weeks and Heritage sent regular updates by email informing her of the progress: "We've received your sample, we've logged in your sample, we are beginning work on your sample." But who really cared? Just give me the darned results, she thought.

CHAPTER TWO

April 29

Kestrel finally had a day off. A life cobbled together from part-time jobs and freelance writing didn't often allow a day with nothing to do.

She didn't think of her day jobs as her career. She was glad to have them, not only to pay the rent, but because they gave her amazing access to the lives and secrets of the most powerful and most insulated people in San Francisco, the very rich. Her astute observations spotted which fortunes were on the wane or whose marriages were on the rocks. Kestrel almost felt like she could make a living telling fortunes. She saw the storms coming before the people swept away with them did.

That information found its way to her blog, SFUndertheRUG.com, to the National Crappers, as she thought of her tabloid clients, and, sometimes, to the real press when she was able to sell a piece to one of the local markets or wire services.

The blog had started as a fun way to use the gossip she gathered to pique the interest of readers and to poke a little fun at the twenty-first-century version of "The Ton," or high society, in San Francisco.

Her network of contacts: maids, nannies, waitresses, shop girls,

Uber drivers, and the invisible army of low-wage workers who support the rich in a wealthy city, guaranteed she knew a lot more about the upper crust than they would be comfortable with. Knowing the players and lending a sympathetic ear paid off. Some of the information she got came from friendship, some from malice, but most she paid for. You can buy loyalty, but not for fifteen dollars an hour and no benefits.

She usually posted to the blog on Monday and the gossip in SF had been skimpy for the past couple of weeks. Sometimes she hated herself for publishing that muckraking little e-rag, but her followers were increasing every month. She didn't delude herself that her readers were drawn by her riveting exposés. She imagined a third of them were looking for salacious gossip about their friends, a third were checking to see what she had written about them (damage control), and the rest were both relieved and miffed to not be included. Didn't P.T. Barnum say, "There is no such thing as bad publicity?" Considering the disruption in her peaceful life made by some of that publicity the year before, she wasn't sure she agreed.

When her mother's distinctive ringtone, Frank Sinatra's "My Way," woke her at ten a.m., she let it go to voicemail. It was always easier to listen to Victoria's messages than it was to speak with her directly.

Kestrel would call, but not right away. There was some perverse satisfaction in making Victoria wait for her to call. She felt like she had spent her whole life waiting for Victoria. To notice her. To care. To whatever it was that would fill the hole in her heart where most people had family. She'd heard from plenty of people that having family wasn't all it was cracked up to be, but when you don't have much, you can't help but think family would be the great panacea, the solution.

Over the years Kestrel's mother had assembled a precarious group of acquaintances, with a constantly changing cast, into something akin to a family. Kestrel had been instructed to call them all Auntie or Uncle, but none of them ever appeared regularly at holiday celebrations. Most holidays consisted of a meal that included Victoria, Kestrel, Grandma McKenzie, and maybe Victoria's latest boyfriend and her best friend of the moment.

Kestrel ran a hand through her tousle of highlighted hair and threw back the covers with a sigh. Thinking about her mother was not conducive to going back to sleep.

She wasn't sure whether you'd call her decor shabby chic, boho, or early thrift store, but she enjoyed her surroundings. Nothing could really alter the vibe she got from the Christmas Story leg-lamp and the rainbow-unicorn squishy pillow she'd recently acquired. She had planned on doing a little housecleaning today but found some comfort in the fact that whatever her mother had in store for her might delay those activities, perhaps for weeks.

Half a pot of coffee, two Pop-Tarts and a long shower prepared her to listen to her messages.

She didn't know why her mother's voice, or maybe it was her tone, sent a frisson of annoyance up her back. "Kestrel? Kestrel? I need you to help me with something. I've called and called. Kestrel? Shit! Call me when you get this. I need you to help me."

She hoped whatever Victoria wanted wouldn't take a lot of her day off. It was likely nothing vital to a normal person.

"Hello, hello?" Victoria's voice sounded weird and kind of muffled over the phone.

"Hey, Mom. It's me. What's up?"

"Where have you been? I need you to come help me with something."

"What's wrong with your voice? I can hardly understand what you're saying."

"Nothing is wrong with my voice, it's my lips."

"Okay, what's wrong with your lips?"

"I just got them plumped and I can't really move them."

"Plumped?"

"Yes, plumped. Just come over and help me, I told you it's hard to talk."

"I can be there in about an hour." Kestrel looked at her watch. If she could get this done early, she'd still have most of her day left.

"Not now, later. Maybe two o'clock."

"Two isn't good for me, Mom. Why can't I come now?"

"Because now isn't good for me." There was a pause of about five seconds and then the inevitable, "You know, I was there for you last year when you got sent to prison."

Kestrel closed her eyes and took a deep breath. "I was in jail one night, Mom, and was never charged. Never mind, what kind of help do you need?" She thought she'd take one last shot at salvaging her day off.

"I'm not supposed to lift anything over five pounds and everything here is a mess. I don't have any food; you need to go to the store."

"You can't go to the store or lift things because you got your lips plumped?"

"No, I can't go to the store or lift things because of the other procedures. I can't go out looking like this." Victoria sighed with exasperation. "Just come over at two."

"All right, two o'clock. See you then." Kestrel ended the call. WTF, what procedures? Victoria was a good-looking woman but she thought and dressed like she was thirty, or maybe eighteen. Victoria took "Forever 21" at its word.

Wan San Francisco sunlight flooded the apartment. She could hear Sam banging around next door, probably trying to tidy all those stacks of books that littered his place. She gave some thought to going over there to help, or to distract him into doing something fun, but decided against it. Sam was many admirable things, but fun was not one of them.

Taking her phone, a notepad, and her coffee cup she wandered out onto the tiny balcony. The potted plants were looking seedy and limp and she stopped to give them a bit of water before sitting down in a dilapidated lawn chair. Her mother insisted on gifting her with various orchids and other needy plantings but, fortunately, Victoria seldom ventured to the duplex on Bay Street and didn't have to witness the lackadaisical care her bequeaths received.

Kestrel scrolled through the messages, deleting the ones from her mother with some satisfaction. One message got her immediate attention. Beatrice, one of her best information contacts, had called. Maybe the day was looking up.

The phone rang three times before Beatrice's breathless voice came on the line. "Hello… hello… Lisbeth, stop screaming, Lucy didn't hurt you. Hello?"

"Beatrice, it sounds like things are hopping at your place. I got your message. What's up?"

"I have some information for you… something I can't talk about on the phone. Can we meet someplace, later today?"

"Sure. I have to go to my mom's this afternoon but I can meet you at that place at the top of Hayes Valley. What time works for you?"

"I'm off work after the twins eat their dinner, how about seven o'clock?"

"That works. See you then."

When she saw that Bobby Burns had called without leaving a message, her finger lingered over the recall button for several seconds before she remembered her vow to stay far away from the police. She thought back over her recent blog posts and couldn't think of any official reason for a call.

She spent what was left of the morning tidying her apartment or pretending to. She'd read Marie Kondo's book on the *Life-Changing Magic of Tidying Up*, but it hadn't really taken hold. She did, however, like to be able to find things when she wanted them, so was occasionally driven to move bits and pieces into appropriate piles.

At one o'clock she made a peanut butter sandwich on raisin bread and wolfed down an individual bag of corn chips. She popped the top on a diet soda and headed out the door for Victoria's home in Sausalito.

She backed the disreputable 1970 VW beetle out of the packed garage and set off. She guessed the car had originally been black, but now it most resembled a dusty blackboard. The engine had been well maintained, though.

At the age of twenty-five, it niggled at Kestrel that she was living on her mother's property and driving her mom's old car, but not enough for her to cut ties, as much as she might want to.

Kestrel had recently discovered that the ubiquitous San Francisco fog had a name, Karl, and today Karl sprawled lazily across the Golden Gate Bridge, spilling from the Pacific Ocean side into the bay side in a great tumble.

The usual mass of walkers, gawkers, and cyclists packed the walkways of the famous bridge. Every second vehicle seemed to be an open-topped bus packed with tourists.

Once off the bridge the fog thinned and sunshine peeked through. She took the Alexander Avenue exit from Highway 101 and followed a meandering path to her mother's Sausalito home where she stopped in the open space in front of the garage. Before she could exit the car,

Victoria was outside standing in front of it, waving her to a different, more secluded spot. Rather than argue, Kestrel just followed Victoria's frantic arm waves to a place well hidden behind the potted plants and windbreak hedge.

Kestrel cranked the car window down. "Hey, Mom. You look like holy hell. What did you have done?"

"Never mind, just be sure you park where nobody can see the car from the road."

"Fine, but why? Who cares whether my beat-up old car is parked here? Afraid it will drag down the property values?"

Victoria looked like she was seriously considering the comment, but then continued to wave Kestrel further into the bushes.

"That's good, you can't be seen there."

"Why does that matter, Mom. Nobody cares if I'm here."

"I care, and I don't want anyone to think I'm home."

"But you *are* home."

"But I don't want people to *know* I'm home."

Kestrel gave up at that point. If her mom wanted to pretend she was not at home, what difference did it make to her?

Kestrel trailed her mother into the living room and was, as always, struck by the multi-million-dollar views from the floor-to-ceiling windows. San Francisco Bay spread out before her, the sparkling water dotted with sailboats, and a killer view of the Golden Gate, including Karl the Fog's creeping sprawl. The house was lovely, but it was secondary to the location, and Kestrel imagined that Victoria received regular letters offering to list her property for untold riches.

Victoria owned several properties in San Francisco, one of which was the duplex on Bay Street. She'd purchased the properties one at a time over several years and remodeled them herself before moving on to another property and renting out the finished space. She had bought the duplex before Kestrel was born, back when it was possible to do so with help from various city agencies.

Now that she had a better look, Kestrel was surprised by the damage done to her mother's face. Her eyes were both blackened with smudges of green and yellow at the outer edges. Her lips looked puffy and painful, and there was some bruising under her jawbone that seriously looked like someone had tried to throttle her recently. Kestrel could totally understand the urge.

"Okay, Mom, I can see why you might not want to go to the local bodega for food, or have friends drop by. What can I do to help?"

"I need you to get me groceries. There's a list on the counter but look in the fridge to see what else I might need."

Kestrel wandered back into the kitchen, opened the fridge, and peered at the sad contents. There were several half-eaten bowls of food, uncovered and still containing a random utensil, dried-out and sometimes unidentifiable.

"Why do you keep all this stuff? You know you aren't going to ever eat it."

"Sometimes I do, and I hate to throw out good food," Victoria said defensively.

"So, what, you wait until it is no longer good and then throw it out?"

"Never mind." Victoria closed the fridge door. "I made a list of things that sound good to me right now. Just go to the store and pick up the stuff. I've got cash for you."

Kestrel picked up the list from the counter, "Canned beef stew, frozen Key lime pie, instant rice, eggs…"

"I'd like some clam chowder, but not that kind you got last time, the good kind."

"I don't know what the good kind is, Mom. Would it kill you to know what brand you like?"

"Just don't get the kind you got last time. If that is all they have, don't get any at all."

"Okay, okay. Is there anything else you need? Coffee, tea, soda, water, whatever?"

"No, just what's on the list."

Bobby Burns called again while Kestrel was on her way to the store. Since she was driving, she didn't pick up, although that usually did not stop her. It did, however, give her a good excuse for not answering.

CHAPTER THREE

April 29

Kestrel was only three items into the list when she received the first call from her mother.

"I just thought of something else I need." Victoria was talking fast, making it almost impossible to understand her.

"Mom, Mom… Victoria! Talk a little slower, remember your lips."

Victoria continued, speaking extremely slowly, "I… need… something… else."

"Okay, you've made your point. What else do you need?"

"Get me some organic blueberries. The middle-sized package."

"Hold on, let me go to produce."

Kestrel made her way through the mass of people to where one tiny woman, wearing a veiled hat, was carefully sorting the best blueberries from several other baskets into the basket she wanted to purchase. It was mesmerizing to watch her inspect each berry before placing it in her tiny basket or discarding it to one of the lesser collections.

"Okay, Mom, they have some little, tiny baskets and they have some bigger baskets but there is no middle-sized basket."

"There must be. They always have the middle-sized baskets."

"Well, maybe the bigger basket is the middle-sized basket because they have sold out of the large baskets."

"What? That doesn't make any sense."

"Never mind, there are two sized baskets. Which do you want? I can get you two tiny baskets, or a large basket and we can dump some of them out."

"You are being ridiculous, Kestrel. Just ask someone if they have any middle-sized baskets."

Kestrel put the phone on mute and glanced around looking for an employee. Not spotting one she waited a few seconds before un-muting. "Okay, the nice lady here got me a special middle-sized basket for you, so I am getting that one." She carefully placed the larger basket in her cart.

There was silence on the other end of the call. Finally, Victoria responded with a distinct sigh, "All right, that's better."

Shopping completed, Kestrel returned to her mother's house, being especially careful to park well behind the hedge, so nobody would know she was there. She carried the bags into the kitchen and swung them up onto the counter.

"How long are you going to be laid up here, Mom?"

"Just a couple of weeks. After this week I can go out with dark glasses to cover my eyes and wear a turtleneck for the other bruises."

"What did you have done? Didn't you just have a lift last year?"

"I just got some Botox last year. This was a little maintenance work." Victoria seemed miffed that Kestrel was keeping track.

"There was nothing that needed work, Mom. It's getting embarrassing that you look younger than I do."

"Well, you know, if you wanted to have a little work done, I would pay for it. Maybe a bit of a tummy tuck, or a little lift around the eyes?"

"Mom." Kestrel wasn't sure how to react. "I'm twenty-five, for God's sake. I think I can afford to wait for a few years to have more work done!" Things were not going as Kestrel had hoped. Better to drop the whole subject before they ended up in an argument that would suck up the rest of her day and all of her energy.

Hoping for a peaceful exit, she opted to change the subject as she put the Key lime pie into the freezer and slid the door closed.

"Did I tell you I that I got a DNA kit to send into Heritage?"

"What kind of a kit did you get?"

Kestrel was busy pouring a generous glass of her mother's Two-Buck Chuck from Trader Joe's and didn't note the icy edge of Victoria's tone.

"You know, one of those things where you mail a vial of your spit to the company and get your DNA results."

"What? What DNA results? How could you do that without asking me?"

Kestrel stepped back against the counter. "I told you I was going to see what came out of it."

"No… no, you didn't tell me that. That's my business, not yours. You have no right to do that!"

Kestrel had seen her mother in a lot of moods, but she had rarely seen her this panicked.

Kestrel placed her hands on her mother's shoulders and pushed her back a step, holding her at arm's length.

"Hold on, Mom. Just relax. Why are you so upset?"

Victoria's breath was coming in gasps. "You have no right to snoop into my business, like that. No right!"

"It's my business, too, you know. I have a right to know whatever there is to know. What are you freaking out about?"

Victoria struggled to gain control of herself. "Nothing."

"Sit down for a minute. What's the big deal? Do you want some wine?" Kestrel took a long slug of her own wine. What the hell was going on here?

Victoria sat down at the kitchen table. Kestrel poured another glass of wine and handed it to her.

Victoria seemed to be thinking quickly, probably coming up with a new spin on the story she had told Kestrel a hundred times.

"What did you get from them? What does it say?"

"I don't know, I haven't even sent it in yet."

"Oh, my God, don't! Just don't even send it." Victoria looked almost hopeful, relieved.

Kestrel took another long slug of cheap wine.

"Promise me you won't send the sample in. Promise me!" Victoria reached out and gripped Kestrel's free hand tightly.

"Mom, I'm not going to promise you anything until you tell me what the hell is going on? Why are you so upset?"

Kestrel considered dropping the whole thing and walking away. She knew that whatever came from this conversation might be better left alone, but she couldn't let it go. For the first time in her life, she might find out the truth, but she wasn't sure she was comfortable with it, whatever it was.

Victoria had turned away from her. "Damned DNA."

"What is it you think I am going to find out, Mom? What lies have you told?"

Victoria seemed to consider all the possibilities. "I don't know what you will find, or not find. I just know you won't find what you expect."

Kestrel pulled out a chair and sat down across from her mother, but not before she finished her glass of white wine and refilled it generously.

"Tell me…"

Conversations with Victoria were never easy, even the simple ones, and this one was grueling. By now Kestrel could almost see the wheels turning behind her mother's eyes. How much should she tell, what had she said before, how little could she get away with revealing?

"I don't know where to start…" Victoria topped off her glass of wine and returned to a different chair at the table, one a little farther away from where Kestrel sat.

"You have a choice, Mom. You can either start at the beginning, like a normal person, or I can ask specific questions and you can try to figure out how to not answer them."

"Very funny… Okay, you ask me questions." She took a healthy swig of wine and a deep breath.

"What are you worried I will find out if I get my DNA done?"

Victoria hesitated and took another gulp of wine, buying time.

"Do I need to make the questions easier?"

"No… I don't know what you will find if you do it. Doesn't it depend on what other people have done?"

"Yes, as does all of life. What is the best I will find?"

"Nothing at all." That at least seemed like an honest answer.

"Okay, what is the worst that I will find?"

Victoria considered her response. "Well, you will probably not find anyone named Paul Jonas."

"And…?"

"And nothing. There is nobody named Paul Jonas, or at least nobody I ever met."

"What does that even mean? Why is this imaginary person named on my birth certificate? Why did you tell me, and everyone else, he was my father?" Kestrel's voice had started to rise.

"I couldn't put 'Unknown' on your birth certificate. How would that look?"

"A lot better than making up some phony name. If Paul Jonas doesn't exist, who is my father?" Kestrel saw the immediate shuttering behind her mother's eyes.

"I can't tell you that."

"You can't, or you won't. Do you even know?"

Kestrel could sense her mother weighing whether she should just say she didn't know and end the discussion but, in the end, she just couldn't bring herself to say it. "I'm not going to tell you. It's my business, and his. Nobody else's."

Kestrel realized she was probably not going to get more from her mother. Her life had been full of this type of stonewalling, but she couldn't seem to let it drop. She wheedled, she begged, she threatened, but in the end she did what she always did and stormed out, slamming the door behind her.

CHAPTER FOUR

April 29

When Kestrel finally left her mother's home, she barely had time to make it to Hayes Valley by seven o'clock to meet Beatrice. She was exhausted and considered skipping the meeting, but she didn't know where to go instead, considering everything that had been undone.

She and Victoria had spent the afternoon hashing over the old stories and the new. Every twisted explanation from Victoria had just opened more wormholes. She'd resisted the lure of opening another bottle of wine when she realized how confused she was getting. By the time she backed the ancient VW from behind the hedge and chugged down the dusty road she was sober, but wished she wasn't.

Hayes Valley was still humming with pre-theater and -opera patrons. Twinkle-lights glittered in the trees, and the street people were rousing themselves to move to a quieter, possibly warmer, place for the night.

She was lucky to find a semi-legal parking place a few blocks from the restaurant and made it only five minutes late for the meeting.

It was easy to spot Beatrice. Tall and striking in a flowing floral dress, her mass of beaded braids pulled into a bundle at the crown of her head, she sat ramrod-straight and slimly graceful on one of the chrome-and-leather barstools. Most of the other customers had wandered in for a quick drink before their evening began, and the room was buzzing.

Beatrice had apparently been there a while and had run up a tab she knew that Kestrel would pick up. Kestrel slid onto the stool next to her. It looked like Beatrice was on Dark and Stormy number three, or maybe four. Kestrel could only hope she would remember what her hot information was.

"Hey, Beatrice, how are you?" Kestrel signaled the bartender.

"Just dandy." She wasn't slurring exactly but the drinks had softened the cadence of her Caribbean accent.

Kestrel ordered two white wines, both for her, and another drink for Beatrice and cut right to the chase.

"Before we get too lubricated, what do you have for me? I'd love nothing more than to get plastered together, but business first." Kestrel smiled, but the dark eyes that turned to her were sad.

"You know I wouldn't talk trash about my people. I'm not that kind of person."

Kestrel waited for her to continue.

The dark woman picked up the fresh drink and then set it down again, gazing at it for several seconds before speaking.

"My whole world is about to go down, and I will be out on the street." She paused. "Not really my world, but my job, and that has been my world for a long time." She picked up her drink, toasted to Kestrel, and swigged down half of it. "There's gon' be him on this side and her on that side, with my babies… the twins," she corrected herself, "all bein' pulled in the middle. That leaves me out in the cold."

Kestrel wasn't fooled. She knew the Jamaican woman loved the little girls and, as far as Kestrel could see, she was the anchor in their privileged existence.

"Do you mind if I take some notes?" Beatrice didn't respond so Kestrel pulled the dot paper notebook and smart pen from her bag. She pressed the "on" button and knew that the pen would record everything said as she jotted down her notes.

Beatrice had always been loyal to "her" family, Theo and Sharon

Spencer and their daughters, and had never been willing to share information about them before. Her professional value to Kestrel had been in the tidbits of information she picked up about the Spencers' friends and social circle. She, like Kestrel, seemed to be invisible to her employers and their friends. Beyond that, Beatrice and Kestrel had been friends since Beatrice had moved to San Francisco several years before. In another mood she was funny, irreverent, and generous. Truth be told, she had been the first to suggest Kestrel start writing a blog. They had bonded over the amazing information they'd gleaned just hanging around the wealthy.

Beatrice glanced around. "No worries, this is straight from the mouth of a totally drunk, pissed-off wife. That fat-ass Theo is dumpin' Sharon for the much younger secretary of his father." Kestrel didn't know if she was more surprised by the news or the language Beatrice was using.

Kestrel's voice dropped to an urgent whisper. "That's a shock." In the Spencers' world the illusion of the solid family and perfect children still meant a lot. Plenty of hanky-panky was going on under the surface but the facade was all-important. She scribbled a few notes to link the recording on her pen.

"Yeah, a shock. Now I'll be out looking for work and I won't be there for my girls." Her voice caught and she swallowed more of her drink.

"But why would they dump you? The girls still need a nanny and you love them."

"Yeah, but the new Mrs. Spencer won't want a nanny who might be sympathetic to the totally screwed ex-wife. They'll just go out and hire one who doesn't know any of the players and doesn't mind kissing the ass of the new mommy."

"What makes you think Sharon won't get the twins and keep you on?"

"What makes you think she wants them?"

Kestrel took a giant swallow of the white wine the bartender had delivered. At least it washed out the taste of what she'd been drinking at her mother's place.

"Okay, say it's true that Spencer wants to hang on to the girls and

Mrs. Spencer wants out of the whole thing, at a price. What does that mean?"

Beatrice smiled. "It means that you will be the very first to announce to the world that Mr. Dickhead Spencer is dumping his long-suffering wife who is willing to sell the twins to the highest bidder." Beatrice's dark eyes were angry and the color in her cheeks had risen.

Kestrel felt some guilt for taking advantage of Beatrice's inebriated state but reminded herself that her friend had been the one who called her. She was the one who wanted to get a little revenge for the betrayal. Good help was not easy to find, and Beatrice was the best. Almost like family… "almost" being the operative word here. Kestrel knew that the woman would have no trouble finding another job in San Francisco. The names of reliable household help were traded about like hot stock tips. It was said that in New York City you watched the obituaries to find an apartment. In San Francisco you watched them to find dependable, vetted staff.

The women moved to a small table and Kestrel ordered some chicken wings and a cheese plate. When she had taken all her notes and the remains of the food were just a few bones, she offered Beatrice cash and, though the woman looked sheepish, she took the proffered bills and tucked them into her purse.

Kestrel knew it was essential to get the news out fast, as it was only hot until the next bit of gossip usurped it. It always surprised her how quickly the shocking scandal of the moment subsided under the stoic determination of the players to carry on with their lives until the new normal was established. Sure, there'd be the "his and her" teams of friends for a while, maybe some temporary exclusion from A-list parties, fancy balls and private luncheons, or ostracism at some of the more elite gatherings. But that would all soon pass, and life would continue along the new path.

Finally, she drove Beatrice to the Spencers' home in Pacific Heights so she wouldn't have to Uber. Kestrel's last words as the nanny exited the car were, "I'll sit on this story until Monday night in case you change your mind."

"Nothing will change…" Beatrice sounded defeated. She turned and walked toward the house, but she stopped for a moment and looked up at the darkened window of the girls' room, only the dimmest glow showing from the unicorn night light. Then she walked unsteadily to the front door and let herself in.

Before she drove off Kestrel quickly typed a Twitter teaser hinting at big news on the Spencer front. She kept her word to Beatrice; after all, a tweet was just a little shout in the wilderness and would disappear if not fed.

There had been some calls: several messages from her mother and another call from Bobby Burns. She didn't have the heart to listen to them tonight. She remembered a bible verse from the vacation bible school her grandmother had sent her to, "...unto each day, its own tribulations." If the overall day hadn't been so messed up, Kestrel might have done a little happy dance over Beatrice's news. As it was, she was lucky to make it home before she ran out of steam.

Her duplex was dark and unwelcoming as she steered the ancient car into the garage. She might have to invest in a unicorn night light of her own to come home to after days like this.

She sat in the dark garage for a few minutes reflecting on how everything could just swerve off kilter with the least little nudge from the universe. How there were things that you knew in the morning that were lies by the end of the day.

She felt like Scarlett O'Hara as she let herself into her dark home and felt her way to the bed before collapsing. "'Fiddle-de-dee... I'll think about it tomorrow. Tomorrow is another day.'"

Through her bedroom wall she felt more than heard the thumping bass of heavy metal music. *Sam must be working; he always plays that when he's working.* She fell asleep with a smile on her face. At least some things never changed.

CHAPTER FIVE

Wednesday, June 9

Grace parked in the below-street-level garage of her condo. After taking the elevator to street level she trekked up a flight of stairs to her front door. She had stopped at Whole Foods on the way home from work and lugged her briefcase, purse, and bagged dinner: some roast chicken, two veggies, and a quinoa pilaf, up the steps.

She plated her dinner, poured some wine, and sat down in front of her laptop. At the top of her emails was the results notice from Heritage. She'd been anxiously awaiting this message but now she wasn't sure. Did she even really want to read it? She felt that opening this can of worms was a lot like being the first one to say "I love you" in a relationship. She checked email, she looked at Facebook and Instagram hoping for something to distract herself, but finally, she logged into the Heritage website.

It took a little while to navigate the site, but finally she found the list of relatives and their "relativeness."

Grace stopped her search. First on the list was a half-brother.

She supposed she shouldn't have been surprised. After all, Grace had been looking for relatives, but, in a way, she guessed she had imagined her birth parents as having dropped off the face of the earth, or at least having stopped procreating, immediately after her birth.

But, no, there was at least one half-sibling, from the paternal side. Heritage only tracked and linked the DNA of people who had submitted samples. There wasn't much information there. Some initials, G.G., and a link to send a contact message. The site didn't look too daunting but absorbing the initial report was about all she could handle right now.

Her hand shook a bit as she reached to shut down her laptop.

She considered snagging another glass of wine from the fridge. Was that what she really wanted? She tried to call her friend Doug but the call went to voicemail. Where was he when she needed him? She'd have to settle for her boyfriend, Kevin. She scrolled to his picture in her contacts and waited anxiously as the phone rang.

"Hey, Kev, how are you, hon?" She tried not to sound too needy, but Kevin was good at sensing people's moods. It paid to know how to respond, whether it was sincere or not.

"Hey, honey." He sounded only a little distracted, probably by some sporting event or other, but she knew it would take just a few seconds to disengage from that and focus on her. There was a reason he was her boyfriend, or friend with benefits. Actually, she wasn't sure what they were. He was cute, fun, hot. He seemed like her ideal match, whatever that meant, and he even acted like he was serious about their relationship from time to time, usually when he was trying to get her to cozy up to his wealthy grandmother. Other times, she felt she was more of an annoyance than a girlfriend.

"I hope it isn't too late to call."

"No problem. How are you?"

"I'm good. Well, maybe not exactly good, but okay." Grace laughed. "I just got these crazy DNA results back today."

"Whoa, what DNA results?"

"I told you. I sent a vial of saliva to Heritage just to see what might turn up."

"Maybe, I'm not sure I remember. Sorry, babe."

"It doesn't matter, it's just that I got the results today, and I'm not really sure how to take them."

There was a pause on Kevin's end. Grace wasn't sure if was related to surprise or beer-opening.

"Kevin?"

"Yeah, babe. Just turning the TV off." Oddly enough, Grace could still hear the game in the background.

"It's pretty surprising stuff. I am seeing a half-brother in here. Not sure how to take it."

"Wow, that's a big deal!"

Bizarrely she could almost hear Kevin thinking this over. What did this mean? What did this mean for Grace? More importantly, what did this mean for Kevin?

"I'm a little freaked out. How do you feel about coming over for a bit? I know it's late, but I could use a little cuddling. Maybe you could spend the night? I could make breakfast in the morning." How desperate could she possibly sound?

"Oh, yeah, that would be awesome, but I'm already in bed and I have a *really* early client tomorrow. Could I get a rain-check?"

Grace's gut-level response was annoyance, but boyfriends were hard to come by in San Francisco.

"No problem. I will talk to you tomorrow." She might have to work a little harder at finding a better boyfriend.

***

Kevin hung up the phone and leaned back against the couch cushions, taking a long pull from the beer bottle he'd just opened.

He'd been thinking that Grace was getting a little boring, demanding a little too much of his attention, but maybe there was something to be said for waiting a bit before dumping her. Besides, his grandmother was smitten with her upper-middle-class pedigree. His folks were gone and he should be a shoo-in for Granny's fortune when she keeled over, but there were all these unspoken requirements he hadn't yet fulfilled: marriage to an appropriate match, children, a real job; the respectable accoutrements of his class.

He worked as a trainer at an upscale gym, which was how he'd met Grace, but Kevin mostly lived off the money he'd inherited when his parents took that accidental right turn going south on Highway One in Big Sur and landed in the Pacific Ocean. He was going through that quickly and would need his grandmother's vast riches to "live in the manner to which he would like to become accustomed." He'd heard that in an old Bugs Bunny cartoon and thought it described his aspirations perfectly.

When they had first met, he'd been impressed with Grace's lifestyle. She'd gone to Stanford, and had a nice condo, plenty of money, a good car… Those things were hard to come by in your twenties in the Bay Area. But he'd learned that, though her parents did all right, they had spent most of their money and energy making Grace's life good, and there would be no huge inheritance when they were gone. Besides, they were healthier than he was and would probably outlive him. Especially if he kept up his own bad habits. He had to admit he was a lazy bugger and couldn't be bothered to see Grace tonight because it would require some effort. Besides, the lean young body lying next to him on the sofa-bed was ever so tempting.

"Was that your girlfriend? What did she want?"

"She needed a booty call, but I told her I was busy."

"Yes, you are…" The eager lips sought his.

Coming up for air, Kevin sighed. "It really is too bad that my grandmother is so set on Grace being the perfect mate for me."

"Fuck them both."

"I'd rather fuck you." Kevin slid down to align himself with the body that was already arching toward him as his head was drawn down for another kiss.

***

Grace hung up her phone and stared out the window for a few minutes. The Victorian houses across the street were a stark contrast to her modern condo complex, but she figured she got the better deal because she got the modern conveniences but her view was of the classic San Francisco homes. Most of them had been converted to apartments long ago, but people kept them up. When Grace first moved in it was disconcerting to have the double-decker tour buses drive past several times a day on the way to Alamo Square but over time it had almost become one of the benefits of living there. Sometimes she'd be unlocking her door with her Whole Foods bags at her feet and the Midwestern tourists would gawk at her like she was a celebrity. If she felt generous, she would wave at them and the tourists would smile and take her picture.

Grace was a little confused about what to do next with her Heritage results. It was different for Doug. He'd wondered all his life who his father was, what might have been if things had been different. But, for Grace, she'd had everything she could have wanted. She'd had her own horse, gymnastics and ice-skating lessons, everything. She had always been told she was adopted, but "adopted" translated to "chosen" and she had been treated that way.

Now there was another family out there. Someone who had not chosen her, but who'd had other children, with other people. Who were they, and why would she want to know now?

She had another glass of wine and went to bed, although it couldn't be said she slept well. What did you do with information that could change your life when your life didn't need changing?

CHAPTER SIX

Thursday, June 24

Grace had been loitering over her final tasks for the day, not particularly interested in leaving the office. Thursday was Kevin's class night, although she'd never been able to quite figure out what class he took, or where it was held. It didn't really matter, but it meant Grace was on her own on Thursdays. She'd delivered the last of the messages she always left at the end of the day when she knew everyone in the East Coast office had already gone home. She would call and ask them questions, and if she were fortunate enough, they would come in Friday morning and return her calls before she arrived at the office. She'd get her answer and would never actually have to speak to them.

As she was checking her social media before heading home, Doug poked his head around the edge of her cubicle.

"Hey, Grace, I just got a call from my dad. He and Corey are going to a drag show in the Castro tonight and they invited me along. Are you interested in going with me? You can be my 'plus one.'"

"Sure, this is Kev's class night and I don't have any plans." Besides, going to a fun event with Doug sounded way more interesting than hanging out in her condo sorting her socks or binge-watching *Bridgeton*, again.

"Want to grab a bite to eat on the way? I think this is just a club and they probably don't serve food."

"Works for me."

She and Doug settled into their seats in the Hayes Street Grill. The restaurant was the place to go before the symphony or opera and they had been lucky to snag a small table toward the back.

"You know, I sent my DNA sample into Heritage a few weeks ago. I got the results back, but I'm not sure what to think of them, or what to do next. There's a half-brother listed."

"That's great, Grace. That is so cool. Are you going to contact him?"

"I might send an email." Grace considered the idea for a moment. "I'd never given it much thought until you contacted your dad. I'm not sure I want to know."

"But aren't you curious?"

"Not really. I have had a great life, great parents. It seems kind of disloyal to even be looking. What if I find something terrible?"

"How terrible could it be?" Doug stopped to place his wine order and Grace signaled him to order the same for her. "If you don't like what you find, you don't have to pursue it. You don't *have* to do anything at all. It's all anonymous unless you want more."

The waiter came and poured the wine. Doug picked up his glass, took a sip and considered for a moment. "For me, I just always wondered who that person, who was the other half of me, was? I still haven't told my mom that I found him. I don't want to hurt her, and I'm sure she was trying to protect me. It just wasn't enough."

Doug paused to order the flatiron steak with fries and Grace ordered the chopped salad. "You are so crazy healthy. Would it really kill you to order the pork belly?"

"No, I believe in moderation, but pork belly just sounds disgusting, like chitterlings."

"What the hell are chitterlings?"

"Pig intestines all cleaned out and fried up. Big deal in the South."

Doug made a face and took another swig of wine. "Whatever, I just like to eat what sounds good. That's probably why I've put on twenty pounds since college."

Grace raised an eyebrow at him over her wineglass.

"Okay, thirty pounds. It looks good on me, I'm big-boned."

Grace laughed. Doug could always make her feel better about things. She decided she wouldn't fret over the Heritage results any more tonight and took another sip of the ruby wine. They were headed to a former church in the Castro district that had recently been made into a club officially named "Spectacles, Testicles, Wallet, and Watch," a bit of homage to the building's liturgical history. The name was a bit long and the acronym STWW didn't really roll off the tongue so it had devolved to "Specs" to those in the know.

The drag show at Specs didn't start until nine p.m. but Doug and Grace showed up a bit early to claim a good table. Grace had never been to a drag show, although she'd lived in San Francisco for several years. The club was dark and filled with small round tables seating two to four people. A long bar ran along one wall and across from the bar was the stage. Three walls were draped with dark curtains and the bar wall was lined with mirror tiles, like a bathroom from the nineteen-seventies. At intervals along the draped walls posters lit by spotlights showed flashily dressed and smiling performers, bewigged and extravagantly made-up. Grace considered for a moment that she looked almost as good as most of them. It just wasn't fair, she thought. But, then again, they probably worked harder at it. At least she didn't have to shave her face every day.

Doug's dad, Kent, and his partner, Corey, arrived around eight-thirty. Grace was intrigued to see that Kent looked remarkably like Doug. He was smartly dressed, wearing khakis and a button-down shirt with a tie. His hair was thin but carefully arranged across his scalp. Corey was the more strapping of the two. He wore jeans and a plaid flannel shirt over a turtleneck. Good quality, but woodsman-like.

Kent greeted her warmly, shaking her hand, and Corey acknowledged her with a nod.

"This show is supposed to be really good. We haven't been here before." Kent glanced around the room eagerly. Corey had already hailed the waiter, who came promptly to get their orders. It looked like they served some limited food options, after all.

Grace and Doug had already shared a bottle of wine and she was glad she didn't have to drive home. She ordered a glass of white, intending to sip it slowly.

Grace wasn't sure whether Doug or Kent was the more excited or uncomfortable around each other. Kent was full of questions, more from nerves than from interest. Doug was happy to answer any and all queries and acted as though letting a silence fall was an inexcusable social faux pas. Fortunately, the show began before Doug had utterly exhausted himself.

Grace was not much of a clubber, and these surroundings were a far cry from Palo Alto. Most of her partying had been suburban college town raves or campus beer bashes. She gazed around her at the array of people. She'd had a couple of glasses of wine with dinner, so she was loving the place, loving Doug's father's wry humor and sly jokes, loving Corey's benevolent sturdiness, loving her friend's excited patter. When the lights in the room went down and the stage lights went up, she was already clapping enthusiastically.

The show was almost over and the waiter had just brought another round of drinks. The finale brought the performers back for a big number with lots of strutting and glitz. Each bedecked and bedazzled songstress had a moment in the spotlight with the other ladies dancing behind her. Grace was impressed with the spectacle and enjoyed watching the stars descend from the stage and sashay around among the tables with the common folk. The performers had begun to retire backstage and the house lights had come up when Grace spotted someone in the crowd. It was just a glimpse really, of a good-looking man escorting the Celine Dion–impersonator offstage, turning to kiss her lightly and putting his arm around her waist before they disappeared behind the curtain. She stared after them for a moment, unsure what she had seen, and then, among the hugs and promises to do this again soon she gathered up her purse and jacket and followed Doug to his car in the misty night. The cool air helped clear her head, but she still felt fuzzy about what she'd observed. Doug asked her if she was okay, and she shrugged off the mood with her best flip of silky hair and a light laugh.

CHAPTER SEVEN

Friday, June 25

Kestrel suspected that if she had a superpower, it was invisibility. Only her unusual name would make her stand out, so her staff schedule said simply, "K. Jones" instead of the more distinctive Kestrel Jonas. The members and guests of the exclusive Pacific Union Club saw only the distinctive braided uniform jacket, trim black slacks and a neat white blouse, ordinary glasses, mousy-brown hair pulled into a tight bun, and functional flat shoes.

She smiled slightly as she topped off the two wineglasses at the corner table. Luncheon service had been over for some time, but she didn't mind staying a bit late to over-serve the two men still lingering over their meal. The two of them had been a gold mine of gossip in the past, although they were oblivious to their role in her blogging career.

One man was stocky and dark-haired, the other was tall, blond, and polished. It was not difficult to differentiate the member from the guest. She had served them both a hundred times but doubted either one could pick her out from the rest of the staff. Kestrel knew a bit of unguarded conversation, a dropped receipt, an ill-timed joke amounted to little to most people, but were valuable nuggets for a careful listener with a big fan base.

She'd initially taken this job to support what she thought of as her journalism career but had quickly learned that there was a lot of information to be gleaned from those who didn't even acknowledge the presence of the service staff.

The elegant Flood Mansion stood at the top of Nob Hill between Grace Cathedral and the Fairmont Hotel. Built in 1886 as the town house of silver baron James C. Flood, it now housed the exclusive Pacific Union Club. The building had resisted the 1906 earthquake and fire as well as the incursion of the twenty-first century; one on-line review summed it up as "no women, no Democrats, no journalists."

***

George sat back in his chair and gazed around the dining room. He never got tired of this place. The ambiance was nice, but his favorite part was that not everyone could come in. You had to belong. You had to be invited to join by a member and it could take years to get approved. Sadly, George knew that he did not have the pedigree to be a member. Garrett Graham, Jr., or Gari, the sleek blond man sitting across the table from him, belonged and probably didn't appreciate it as much as George did. It took an outsider to get a thrill from the privilege it afforded.

Gari continued talking but George was not really listening. Another aspect of privilege was the belief that people cared what you said, and that belief was deeply ingrained in Gari. George had lost interest somewhere between the gripe about the kids' private school woes and who from the Bohemian Club was going on the Concerts and Castles cruise next summer. He glanced at his watch. Almost two p.m. He'd told his admin that he was in a client meeting, but somebody was going to have to pay for the fifteen-minute increments and he could only slip so much into each of the accounts before someone noticed. But Gari had no place to be, so on he droned.

When George had married Gari's sister, Amélie, spelled in the French way, he'd assumed he would have no trouble fitting into society as understood in San Francisco. He wasn't old money, but he had married it, and he had a law degree. He'd imagined his days would be more like his brother-in-law's: work out at the club, a long lunch, a squash game, and shower before heading home for a gourmet meal. But, surprisingly, Amélie was not that kind of rich. Oh, the money was there, but she controlled it, and George, with an iron fist. He had the credit cards and the bank account access, but Amélie and Bertram, their accountant, spent hours going over every purchase to assure they knew where the money went. Bertram was only a cousin, but you'd have thought every ducat was coming out of his own pocket.

He pictured Amélie carefully reviewing his credit card statements, sighing and making little disapproving sounds. "Honey, can you clarify this three-hundred-dollar charge to the Fairmont? Was it necessary to spend quite so much for Gari's birthday lunch last month? You and he are not that close," or "I see you've started shopping at Brooks Brothers again. Should I give the store a call and ask for a more itemized list of the charges?" To be fair, Amélie was very aware of the limits of the money she'd received from her mother. They would need the infusion of cash from her father's estate before long.

It had become a game for George to figure out how to slip little things past their scrutiny and retain a small cache of money in the locked bottom drawer of his office desk. Any legitimate ATM purchase that afforded the chance for a cash payout was taken advantage of. Expensive gifts of items he didn't need were quickly converted to cash, and, so far, nobody had noticed the little knick-knacks disappearing from their homes after George visited. If they did notice they chalked it up to the staff. It gave him a hit of satisfaction to slip some ludicrously expensive piece of crap into his pocket.

It stung that he was the only person in their social circle who held down a nine-to-five job, except for his boss, Dixon, who ran the firm but he had old money as well. Early on Amélie had made it sound noble and manly to be the breadwinner of their little family, so that everyone would know he hadn't married her for her money. Yeah, some of their friends had offices and secretaries, but the secretaries were cute young things who mostly answered the phone and told callers that "Mr. So-and-so is out of the office this afternoon. May I take a message?"

Shit! Gari was looking at him expectantly. George leaned forward.

A look of concern plastered on his face. He suspected the soliloquy had veered to the ongoing challenge to the Graham trust. Gari's face had gone from its usual pasty white under the spray tan closer to crimson, progressing to purplish at the roots of his carefully styled blond hair.

"Could you run that by me again, I don't think I got it all?"

"I said, some by-blow of my dad's has shown up on Heritage."

"Really?" This may have been the first time Gari had ever said anything that shocked George.

"Yes, really. It couldn't come at a worse time."

"I thought the court thing was pretty much settled."

"It is but, guess what? This could really throw everything off."

"Isn't there something in the law about legitimate kids and bastards?"

Gari looked at him with disdain. "You tell me, you're the attorney."

"That's not fair, I'm in tax law, and you know it."

"If dear Dad had left the money directly to us, it would probably not matter, but he didn't. He left it to a bunch of charities. But since we claim he was loony-tunes and are trying to overturn the will, this chick may have just as much claim as we do."

Gari picked up his wineglass. "If she finds out who we are, she could take a quarter of it all."

Gari had finally managed to get George's full attention. The whole family had figured the lawsuit to override the old man's trust would be a slam-dunk and none of them had been more anxious to get their share than George and Amélie. The money from Amélie's mother had been nice, but Garrett, Senior's holdings were worth a hundred and fifty million, maybe more. Split between the three legitimate kids, it had been well worth fighting for.

"I thought about getting in touch with her and offering her some money to just disappear, but that might just make her suspicious."

"Who is she, is she here in San Francisco?"

"I don't know anything about her. Just an email through Heritage saying it looks like we're related, and she'd love to know more." Gari paused for a moment. "Goddamn Mary for sending that sample in. She must have hoped we were related to royalty or something." He recalled when Mary, his wife, had insisted he spit into that infernal tube. "The kids need this for their family tree project at school," she had argued.

George realized his wineglass was still full, or full again, and picked it up. "Maybe you could have someone else approach her and offer some money. I mean, without really letting her know who you are."

"Maybe, I don't know. Who could do that for me? This is sensitive. I haven't even mentioned it to the girls."

George thought calling his own wife and her sister Bridget "the girls" was a bit of a stretch. They hadn't been girls in a while, no matter how much money they spent on trainers, spa weeks, hairstylists, and cosmetic surgeons.

George just sat back and took another large sip of wine. Gari was not the brightest bulb in the marquee, but you could almost hear the wheels turning in his head. Five, four, three, two…

Right on cue Gari's head swiveled in George's direction.

"Hey, you could do it for me. You could just go feel this half-sister out and see what you think."

"Oh, I don't know, I'm not sure I'm really the right person for the job." *Don't protest too much, you have him on the line now.*

"Sure, you are. It would just be to see what she's like."

George pretended to be considering the proposal, but it was difficult to hide his interest in Gari's dilemma.

"I guess I could meet her and just say I am a friend of the family. No mention of money, or anything."

"Yes, that would work. I need to know what I'm dealing with here."

"Why don't you forward me the email she sent and I'll think about it."

"Sure, sure…" Gari seemed to relax a bit and glanced at his watch.

"Hey, it's almost two-thirty. I have a squash game in half an hour." Gari stood up.

"What kind of money are you talking about, if it works out?" *Don't sound too anxious, lame ass.*

"I don't know, it could be worth a hundred thousand to me. Of course, you'd get a fee, as well."

George stood up and tried to look nonchalant. "Okay, I'll give it some thought."

George turned back before leaving the club. "We are on for the Bohemian Club spring picnic on Saturday, right?"

"Yeah, we'll pick you up about eight-thirty in the morning. All this crap takes the fun out of it, though."

As George stepped out the door, he saw the cable car reaching the top of the crest and waited several seconds for it to disgorge its gaggle of tourists. He headed toward his office with a much lighter step knowing that some of the gawkers were sure to have seen him exiting the elite Pacific Union Club. He'd have been surprised to know that most of them had no idea the PU Club even existed.

One hundred thousand dollars! It was a drop in the bucket compared to the inheritance that was at risk. A fortune split three ways beat a four-way split any day. George had plans for Amélie's money and was not the least interested in sharing it.

***

Gari headed across toward the Fairmont and on to the nearby gym for his squash game. It had been easier when the squash courts had been right at the club, but it was a beautiful day, so the walk wasn't bad.

The discussion with George had resurrected the humiliation of the reading of his father's will; the realization that his old man had kept a tally on each of his children over the years. Private school tuitions, uniforms, music and dance lessons, traffic tickets, college expenses, weddings, ski trips, house down payments, club memberships, minor legal scrapes …everything. Then, after Mom was gone, he'd moved into The Towers, that concrete pile at the top of the hill, to retire and buy his redemption of a misspent life by allocating the remainder of his wealth to religious and charitable organizations. The attorney had handed each of them a tabulated listing recapping the minutiae of their fiscal lives and noting the exact amount of the trust funds they each had from their mother. Gari was embarrassed for all of them, but, more than that, he was furious. This hadn't been the implied agreement, the deal he had made by living his whole life to the plan his father had dictated. The private schools, the violin lessons, the right college. All of it was to satisfy his part of the bargain, and his parents' side of the deal was that the money and houses and paintings and "stuff" would eventually go to the perfect children they had raised.

What different choices would he have made if he'd known he had options? Would he have pursued a different career, married a different woman, had a different life? He'd done what he thought was necessary; and yet, here he was, fighting in court for what should have been his, and all the time his father had been screwing around leaving little bastards here and there.

Even the attorney had been chagrined by the whole thing. Hell, he'd known them all since they were babies. He'd mumbled something about trying to talk Garrett, Sr. out of this plan. Finally, after asking them if they had any questions, he provided them with the name of an attorney in the firm who specialized in trust-busting.

At the gym he slammed the locker door and picked up his squash racquet and water bottle. This ought to be a great game; he felt as if he could kill someone. Poor Archie. Gari only had to imagine he was playing against his father to make this game a massacre.

CHAPTER EIGHT

Friday, June 25

George returned to his office late. The hell with the billing. He'd just add the extra hour to the various clients who had money to burn. For now, he was stunned over what he had learned. He'd get in touch with Gari's bastard sister and see what she wanted, and maybe, if he was lucky, she just wanted to update her family tree. Maybe he could pass himself off as Gari. Maybe he'd have to cough up a few thousand bucks, but she didn't have to know about the Graham fortune. This didn't have to be the debacle Gari was making of it.

He checked with his admin for messages and then locked himself in his office. At his desk he unlocked the bottom drawer. Everything that he owned that was his alone was there. Some cuff links from his in-laws that would eventually be turned to cash, about forty-five hundred dollars, and a few odds and ends he had lifted from here and there. There, too, was the sales brochure for the winery in Napa. He pulled it from the drawer and spread it open on his desk. When he couldn't sleep at night, he lay awake and imagined a life like that. Finally, he'd be able to make his own mark, but it all depended on winning the lawsuit.

Sitting back in his chair he picked up the framed photo of his perfect little family from his desk. That photographer had been a genius. In the picture George beamed, Amélie gazed adoringly at him, and their two children, who minutes before had been arguing bitterly, smiled brightly.

He replaced his possessions, carefully locked the drawer, and spent the rest of the afternoon browsing through file folders and duly billing his long lunch in chunks to all the pertinent folks. When it got close to five o'clock he locked his office and headed for home.

He had to admit that he truly enjoyed going down to the parking garage, claiming his Mercedes from his reserved space and heading for home. Home was a different issue. The house was beautiful, thanks to his wife and her money, but he didn't feel like much of it was his. Amélie would be waiting, dinner would have been provided by the private chef, and, if he was lucky the kids would have already eaten and taken their iPhones to their rooms. The wine would be perfect, the beef rare, the asparagus still crisp, and Amélie, still as disappointed as ever.

Whenever George felt stifled, he remembered how flattered he'd been by Amélie's initial adoration when they first married. It was too bad that he wasn't equipped to give her the husband and father she'd hoped he'd be. You weren't just born with those skills. He always felt like he was falling short of expectations, but when they got their money, he'd talk her into fulfilling his dreams. When he was doing interesting work he loved, he'd be a better husband and father.

As usual, Amélie was perfectly groomed. What was that saying about putting lipstick on a pig and it still being a pig? That wasn't really fair. Amélie was fine. She was always perfect and perfectly correct. There were no complaints. Other than they both had been horribly misled and disappointed by who they each actually were. If George were being fair, he would have to admit that Amélie got the worse end of the deal. He'd been in law school, not bad-looking, obsequiously appropriate to her family, and anxious to marry someone who doubted herself enough to fall for his line of BS. Part of Amélie's problem was that she didn't much value what was good about her: her intelligence, her tenacity, her willingness to compromise, and she over-valued the attributes of a pretty face, big boobs, and a coquettish personality, which she definitely did not possess. As a result, George had scored high on the stepping-up-in-the-world scale.

George was not exactly low class. If anything, he was classless. Thanks to a middle-class upbringing with the added benefit of a bequest from a relative that allowed for private school, college, and law school he'd been well situated to step up in the world. He didn't exactly rock his education, but he took advantage of it. His private school experience introduced him to the people who were in the upper echelon of San Francisco society. He was funny, handsome, charming, and just devious enough to make him a convenient connection. If you needed some drugs, or some girls, or almost anything else, George was "the guy". Sometimes he didn't have the connections he claimed, but he would do his best to assure you got what you wanted, legal or not. He had more intelligence than people gave him credit for, those people being defined as the gang he clung to through school.

The fateful day he met Amélie Graham in advance of the San Francisco Cotillion, was mostly due to his willingness to BS wherever necessary. The Cotillion was always on the lookout for escorts and Gari had suggested he volunteer. It wasn't truly the first time he and Amélie had met, but it was the opportunity he'd waited for. He'd admired her poise and brains but hadn't seriously thought he'd have a chance with her.

There weren't still many places in the country where a cotillion or "coming out" made any difference, but to some few in San Francisco, it was their chance to score big in the marriage market, and many secretly felt George had done so.

Before going to his office the next day George would stop by the San Francisco public library on Larkin Street. He'd log into his unofficial email address and find that Gari had forwarded the link he needed from Heritage.com.

It was straightforward. He'd send a quick note, indicating enthusiasm and a little excitement at meeting a newly discovered sister. When, where, and how could they meet? Can't wait to hear the details. Completely open, except that George was not the half-brother who had been contacted. He was the brother-in-law desperate to protect the family fortune.

CHAPTER NINE

Friday, June 25

Kestrel finished clearing the dishes from the table and reflected that she could probably strip naked and run through the Pacific Union Club and none of them would be able to identify her. Her manager might remember her name, "Kay Jones, or something like that," he would say.

She was very good at this job, as she was at all her jobs. People didn't bother to remember good service; it was the fuckups that stayed in their brains. The only personal Yelp review she'd ever garnered had come from a matronly woman who objected to her service taking too long that time Kestrel had fallen down the back stairs.

In the kitchen she quickly disposed of the dishes and ducked down the hall into the locker room. She punched out fifteen seconds after the end of her shift. You never wanted to become visible to the bookkeeper.

Her shift at the PU Club completed, she only needed to get through dinner at The Towers. It was just a fifteen-minute walk to the next gig so she skipped the bus.

On her way to The Towers Kestrel had, at first, kept her head down, lost in her thoughts, but her natural curiosity soon had her watching the behavior of the people on the street. She stopped a few times to drop some change into the cup of a veteran, a runaway, or a soundly sleeping street person propped up against a downspout. As she crossed California Street against the traffic the honking horns caused a man going into a doorway to glance around nervously. Initially she hadn't noticed him, but the furtive movement caught her attention. Holy shit, it was that slimeball Ogden Norwich, and the woman beside him was not his wife. Her unerring gossip antennae began to tingle.

The dark little hotel would be hard to follow them into, but she had her ways. She ducked into a disused entryway and using the grimy window in the door as a mirror she took the clip from her hair and shook out the heavily frosted mass of hair that the tidy bun disguised. It didn't take long to stow her hoodie and glasses in her gym bag and remove her white blouse, revealing the strongest element of her disguise; the size 36-D breasts that had been an eighteenth- birthday gift from her mother. Snuggled into a low-cut, body-hugging camisole, they drew the attention of men and women alike. If nothing else, Victoria's early insistence that Kestrel's flattish chest needed some enhancement had benefited her at times like this. It might not be the birthday present most girls received, but it was one of the few times she'd succumbed to her mother's wheedling; something she'd sworn not to do again. It was not as difficult to disguise as some might think. Sports bras and loose clothing were a great help in that department.

Next, she slipped out of her work shoes and comfy socks and drew a pair of four-inch strappy heels from the bottom of the bag. They were worn so seldom the trademark red leather Louboutin soles were still pristine. She applied a gash of velvety matte scarlet lipstick, fluffed her hair as well as her bosom and added a pair of Gucci dark glasses.

It wasn't until she turned back to the street that she noticed the gawping transient comfortably ensconced in the dim stairwell. She gave him a devilish grin and pulled a five-dollar bill from her pocket and placed it on the step next to him.

Drawing herself up to her full five-eight height and throwing back her shoulders she zipped her bag and followed Ogden and his lady friend's path into the dim hotel lobby. Her transformation had taken longer than she'd thought and she hoped they had not already disappeared into the elevator.

This was her favorite vocation, finding out all the dirt on the high and mighty and thinly disguising it on SFUndertheRug.com. She had wanted to be a serious journalist but those jobs were hard to come by. Then she'd read that gossip sheets had a long and well-documented history of entertaining the wealthy. They were common in nineteenth-century British high society; the TV show Bridgerton even had a main character who laid bare the secrets of "The Ton." Hell, they had probably existed in ancient Egypt. She could imagine a papyrus scroll being passed around with all the dirt on King Tut.

The website name could have used some work, but, once she started publishing it and got some buzz, changing the name would have confused everyone. For now, all of San Francisco, or at least the ones who mattered, read what she posted and either gorged on the evisceration of their friends or secretly bemoaned not being interesting enough to get written up. Staying under the radar and mousy-looking had served her well. At first the clubs and restaurants, the hotels and bars, the sex shops and porn theaters had been appalled at being mentioned in the shenanigans going on in the shadows. But they soon figured out that people flocked to see and be seen there, so they paid to advertise with her. She made much more from those endorsements than she ever would from her menial jobs, but the lowly jobs provided unending fodder for the masses. Technically, she didn't need any added support from her mother, but it suited her to have Victoria underestimate her.

Up to this point, only the SFPD had any clue that she wrote the blog, and that had been a disastrous discovery for everyone, especially Kestrel and the police commissioner.

What had started as an innocent observation of some clandestine meetings had blossomed into a full-fledged scandal that toppled more than one career and embarrassed many powerful people. At one point Kestrel had been on the mayor's personal hit list, but she had turned out to be the least of his problems.

At some point she would have to admit to Victoria that she wasn't dependent on her mother's largesse, but that time was not yet. It suited her to maintain their financial connection as one of the few they had.

Once inside the dim lobby it took a few seconds for her eyes to adjust. There was Ogden trying to look like a city titan at the same time he tried to hide behind the young woman at his side. Not an easy task for someone who'd put on some weight in the last few years. The girl was young enough to be his daughter, but she was not. Ogden had only lunky sons who looked and acted much like he did. Maybe she was his trainer. She was wearing hip-hugging yoga pants and a sports bra under the leather coat that she kept trying to remove and that he kept slipping back up onto her shoulders. Kestrel suspected his hungry wolf expression when he looked down at her was not admiration for her athletic ability, or maybe it was. Kestrel had her phone out and had taken a couple of distance shots but wanted to get close enough to hear their conversation. No problem, she'd served Ogden dozens of times at the PU Club, but he was never going to recognize her. She walked quickly up to the desk and acted as though she was waiting her turn to speak to the clerk.

"I thought we were going to get something to eat first," the trainer whispered.

"We are. We are going to have lunch with champagne sent to the room." Ogden kept his voice low, but Kestrel was very close.

The trainer did not look impressed and started to say something.

"And, I have a little surprise for you." He patted his jacket pocket and waggled his eyebrows at the girl.

"Excuse me," Kestrel interrupted. "I just need to ask a quick question and I will be on my way." Her entitled attitude in interrupting them was the finishing touch to her disguise.

She turned to the clerk. "Do you have a catering menu for the private ballroom? I am thinking of having a little party and just love the ambiance here."

The clerk rummaged through the desk and came up with a dog-eared menu. As Kestrel turned toward the couple, she noted that Ogden's gaze was fixed on her breasts. She glanced at him, and then meaningfully at the trainer, who had also noticed Ogden's attention had drifted. For a moment their eyes locked and Kestrel easily read the meaning behind the trainer's tight smile.

The young woman slipped her arm possessively around the man's waist and they turned toward the elevator as Kestrel pretended to study the catering menu.

Once out of the dark entry and into the street Kestrel sent another quick tweet out to the gossip-hungry hordes; this one accompanied by a dim photo of an obvious hotel desk.

A few of her friends who knew about the blog had asked her why she had it in for the wealthy, and she had given it some thought. She didn't really dislike them. Okay, maybe she did sometimes, but it was really what she perceived as their sense of entitlement and superiority when underneath they were doing all the same crap the poor were doing, maybe worse. Her fifth-grade teacher, seeking something positive to report in a parent-teacher conference had stated, "Kestrel has a very developed sense of justice."

CHAPTER TEN

Friday, June 25

When Kestrel reached The Towers, it took a bit of time to undo her disguise, or maybe re-do her disguise. Sometimes she wasn't sure which one was really her. Was she the mousy waitress, the sly muckraker, the dutiful daughter, or someone else completely?

The bun that hid the bleached highlights took several minutes to accomplish and, unfortunately, the high-end matte lipstick lived up to its kiss-proof advertising. By the time she'd scrubbed most of it off she looked as if she'd been smacked in the mouth. When she was done, she clicked the replay button on the phone. "I thought we were going to get something to eat first..." the voice whined. Perfect. With her cloak of invisibility firmly in place she stowed her bag and headed for the dining room.

San Francisco Towers is a very exclusive "life-plan community." Aging people with a lot of money buy in as owners and pay substantial monthly fees for all the services, including cleaners and meals. They start out in apartments, move on to assisted-living, and eventually graduate to skilled nursing before they finally die off and their space is sold to someone else. The buy-in is upwards of a million dollars that disappears over a few years (it's not like you can bequeath the apartment to your kids) and there is a lengthy waiting list. But the art hanging on the walls is loaned from local museums, the staff is courteous and helpful, the food is chef-created, and you can even have a little roof garden of your own.

She was fifteen minutes early for her shift. Plenty of time to look over the menu and dining room before the influx of early birds; those little old men and women who had begun to dress for dinner at three p.m. Jacket and tie, no jeans, walkers at the ready, they were already beginning to congregate in the vestibule, eyeing the menu board suspiciously.

"What the hell is vich-ee-swas?" a voice quavered over the low murmur in the room. "What?" it queried again.

Another, slightly clearer voice repeated, "Cold potato soup, dear."

"Sounds terrible. Do I like it?"

Kestrel's uniform for this gig was more like hospital scrubs. Dark blue, neatly ironed, not too new. White stitching on the breast pocket, *K. Jones.*

Casper, her manager, pulled her aside in the kitchen, "Miss Jones, you'll be serving the private dining room this evening. Mrs. Durbin is having a little family gathering. Elvin will give you the menu and wine instructions." After a pause, he continued, "There will be a number of children, and some teenagers, I believe." His voice held a hint of sympathy for her, but she was thrilled.

The extended Durbin family was a font of gossip and juicy information. She would know many of their nastiest secrets before the evening was through: who hates whom, who sleeps with whom, which teens are taking drugs, which are dealing drugs. It was a gold mine, but fraught with landmines. She was torn between wanting to expose the juicy tidbits and protecting the simply naïve.

Dinner in the private dining room was more to protect the other residents than to make the party exclusive. The dress code was a little looser for diners, it required a little more service from the staff, and it might involve cutting and distributing a cake. Lilah Durbin would have arranged to bring her own wine as The Towers didn't provide it.

Lilah Durbin was the last in a long line of early San Francisco families who had started out as madams and conmen on the grift for a quick fortune during the Gold Rush and, with a little luck, and a lot of grit, had become the millionaire scions of San Francisco. Kestrel had spent a lot of time researching the Durbin family history last year and had run a series of blog posts revealing the dark deeds and fancy dealings that got them where they were. She liked Mrs. Durbin and sincerely hoped the blog posts had not contributed to her recent stroke. She preferred to think that Lilah Durbin had gotten a kick out of the exposé of her family's past. Besides, nobody really cared what your old granddaddy did for a living as long as the gold flowed downhill to the next generation. She knew that Lilah had only one child, who only had one child. The children and teens at this gathering were the offspring of hangers-on nieces, nephews, and honorary family members. Kestrel hoped they weren't just there for the money that Lilah would leave behind when she shuffled off this mortal coil. Kestrel thought of her as being like the "Unsinkable Molly Brown": down to earth, strong, with a keen eye for bullshit. She wasn't above a bawdy tale after a glass, or two, of wine, and she could laugh at herself and those around her with equal glee. Tonight, Lilah looked especially delighted that her only grandson and his fiancée were her special guests. In her research Kestrel had found that their relationship hadn't always been smooth, and she'd never seen him at one of these private dinners before. He had taken the seat next to his grandmother and seemed to have stepped into the role of toastmaster for the event. She got that feeling in her gut that was a cross between a tingle and a gas pain that usually meant she would be well served to do a little background check on him. Half of the success of her blog had been from following up on those special feelings she sometimes got when she met people.

Grace, the fiancée, seemed sweet, quiet, maybe a little intimidated by the large gathering of strangers, but she spoke kindly and listened with intense interest to Lilah's stories. Kestrel got no tingle when she saw her, but she did wonder how it was she managed to get hooked up with the Durbin fortune. Watching her, Kestrel thought maybe if she kept herself up as nicely as Grace, she could snag a fortune as well. They didn't look that much different.

Managing the party entailed subtly accompanying the teens to the restrooms as they periodically ducked out for a smoke or whatever they got up to when they escaped the family's eagle eyes. Making sure they got back to the table without wandering into the rest of the facility kept Kestrel busy.

The only flaw in her carefully choreographed dinner service was when one of the teens decided to drop his napkin and take a grab at her ass as she retrieved it. Under normal circumstances she would have knocked him sideways, but she caught herself in time and sidestepped his grope. Her uniform was not baggy, but she wore it loosely enough to disguise the curvier portions of her figure. It was clear he would probably have grabbed at anyone who bent over.

When the last of Lilah's guests had departed and Kestrel was tidying up the table before clocking out, Lilah still sat at the head of the table with a final glass of wine. She smiled at Kestrel. "Why don't you sit down and talk to me for a minute, have a glass of wine?" It was not unusual for Kestrel and Lilah to find themselves the lone inhabitants of an empty dining room.

"Let me clock out and I will come back and talk, but no wine. It wouldn't do for you to be seen drinking with the staff."

When Kestrel returned, she pulled a chair up close to the table and let Lilah do the talking. She suspected the older woman didn't have many confidantes and she would never use what she heard from her on the blog. Kestrel just liked talking to her. Lilah was thoughtful tonight as she sipped her wine. "You know, I was a waitress one summer. Don't look so surprised. My daddy thought it was a good idea for me to get a taste of what he called 'how real people lived.'" She shook her head and smiled. "I was a truly terrible waitress: couldn't keep the orders straight, spilled things on people. It was just awful. It did make me appreciate good service, though."

Lilah leaned back and gazed into the middle distance, distractedly swirling the last of the wine in her glass.

"I don't know why I keep having these dinners. I don't really like the people that much and I suspect they don't care for me."

When Kestrel started to protest, she put her hand up to silence her. "Don't argue with me. If I can dislike them, they are perfectly free to dislike me. We are not a close family and I suspect they all show up so that when I die, they'll be included in my will. My grandson is the worst. Can't wait for me to keel over."

"I'm sure that isn't so, Mrs. Durbin. He seemed very happy to be here tonight."

"Well, yes. He was happy to be invited again, and I was happy that he came with that lovely girlfriend of his. I keep saying fiancée, but I don't think they are that serious. I just wish they were. He is pretty much the last hope I have of leaving a legacy beyond wealth. I'd love to see him have a family before I kick the bucket."

Kestrel didn't know what to say and wasn't about to agree with someone whose next-day sober feelings toward the family might be much more benign.

Again, there was a long pause while Lilah finished her wine. "I wish I had Garrett Graham's guts. I'd just leave the whole estate to worthy causes. You know he did that, right?"

"Well, I heard something about it." It was only the biggest scandal of the past year. Kestrel knew that Lilah Durbin and Garrett Graham had been neighbors at The Towers, and friends since childhood.

"He was, in the end, fed up with their selfishness, and expectations." Lilah paused for a moment. "Of course, some part of that was probably making up for his own debauched existence." Another pause. "Too bad they are contesting the will and trying to prove he had diminished capacity. Did you know the attorneys came and talked to me? They wanted me to say he was crackers at the end, which he may have been, but I wasn't about to tell them that. I told them he was the sanest person I ever met." She chuckled quietly. "Now they are probably investigating my sanity."

"If you had it all to do over again, what would you do differently?" Kestrel asked.

Lilah answered more quickly than expected. She'd obviously been giving this some thought. "I'd have had more children and made less money. We tried to have more babies, but it just didn't happen and what good is all that money to me now? It can't even buy my family's love."

After a moment, Lilah placed her empty glass on the table and pushed her chair back. "Could you please get someone to escort me to my apartment?"

"Of course, Mrs. Durbin." Kestrel went in search of someone to help. She was always amazed at how fucked up even the wealthiest families were, but she hoped that Mrs. Durbin's wishes for her grandson came true.

CHAPTER ELEVEN

Friday, June 25

It was eleven p.m. when Kestrel got home and she was anxious to post her hotel encounter with Ogden Norwich and his trainer. She'd already been composing the entry to her blog while she was on the bus.

Most days did not have two shifts and an early-morning writing session, so she was beat. Her side of the duplex was dark, but she could see her neighbor, Sam, lumbering past the kitchen window in the other unit.

His door opened as she pulled her key from the pouch on her hoodie. The night had become damp and chilly, and she was anxious to get inside. "Just taking out the garbage," he said and lifted the two bulging plastic bags for her to see. "Want me to take yours out?"

"Sure, just a second and I'll get it." She probably should have asked him in, but she had tolerated too many people today and just wanted to be alone. She grabbed her garbage and recycling bags from the kitchen and pulled the drawstrings tight, only slightly embarrassed by how much of her recycling was fast food containers and wine bottles.

While he wrestled the four bags down the driveway, she grabbed her mail from the box, stepped inside and closed the door before he got back. She did have the good grace to call, "Thank you, Sam" over her shoulder as the door closed and the entry light went on.

She stood inside the door and sorted through the mail. "Junk, junk, bill, junk, check, yes!" she murmured. The National Crapper had finally paid her for the last article. It was amazing how fast the tabloids could smear a dead celebrity on their front pages, lurid pictures and all, and how long it took them to pay the writer for the shit they had smeared them with.

She opened her laptop and downloaded the pictures and the recording from her phone and, when her gaze found its way to the counter where the open bottle of wine lurked, she firmly turned back to her story. Ogden might remember someone being at the counter, but he'd never be able to place her. She had no idea if anyone else had spotted the little tête à tête, but she wanted to be the first person to spread the word. Of course, she didn't use his name, or name the hotel, specifically. Thanks to photo software she could blur the faces. There would be a fair amount of speculation around the tables of the ladies-who-lunch group tomorrow, but the key players would know exactly who she was talking about. Early on with the blog, she'd worried that someone might take her to court, until she realized that they would have to admit they were the person in the article, and they weren't about to do that.

When she had posted the story and pictures on the blog page, she thought a bit about the previous year's posts that had shaken San Francisco from the foundations to the top of the hierarchy.

It had started as just another observation of unlikely folks getting together in unusual places, but had evolved, or maybe devolved, into a scandal that was still reverberating through the city. Random sightings of the city's most powerful, wealthiest, and most influential mingling and whispering with the shadiest elements, combined with a minimum of city-records research revealed a web of collusion, bribes, and other shenanigans that had embroiled her in a fight she hadn't counted on when she blithely posted them on the World Wide Web.

That was the first time Kestrel had felt she might have a real nose for news. Digging up dirt on entitled people she didn't like anyway had been entertaining, fun, and lucrative. But it had been exhilarating to discover a real cover-up, and the machinations of the powerful had angered her at a profound level.

She poured herself a tall red wine before she sat down with a pad and pencil to listen to the messages on her phone.

There were a couple of her city connections with juicy tidbits to share for a price, several blank messages, the happy announcement that she had won an all-expense-paid cruise to someplace, and a whiny missive from her mother.

She zapped the Mommy message away halfway through. They were always the same. *Blah, blah, whine, poor me, ungrateful, blah, blah, blah.* She should probably be more appreciative. Before her blog took off she'd have been living in some basement in South San Francisco if her mom didn't own this duplex and let her pay lower rent. Not free, mind you, but at least affordable. Mom would be the first to tell you that she couldn't afford to give it away, but she was mostly gracious, especially early on, when the rent had been late. Well, hell, she'd call her Saturday, or maybe Sunday.

The fact that her own bank account had been rapidly growing, and she'd even ventured into the world of investing, was confusing. On one hand her mother would have been happy to hear about her success, but on the other, if Victoria didn't think she had a financial hold over Kestrel, what relationship did they even have? Victoria liked being in charge and needed some power, even if it was just the purse strings she controlled. Kestrel was loath to let her mother know of her own independence. She did not want her mother to know she wrote the blog. Victoria read it voraciously, and often commented on it. It took some self-control not to admit that she wrote it, but it was Kestrel's little ace in the hole. As long as her mother thought she worked shit jobs for low pay and could complain about having paid for her college education, they at least had something to talk about.

It was too late to call her contacts back, even though one of the items sounded promising. It seemed there was trouble in paradise in one of the more refined homes in SF.

She threw out the ads, opened the bill. Tomorrow she needed to go online and set this up for electronic billing. Nobody got paper bills anymore.

Finally, she opened her emails. There, right at the top was a message from Heritage.com. Her DNA results. She had been drunk and pissed at her mom when she ordered the kit, sober but still pissed when she spit in the tube and mailed it back. It seemed like it had been months since then. How come the crime shows on TV could do all the analysis and solve the crime in an hour and it took four to six weeks to analyze her sample? She was no longer particularly pissed as she poured herself another glass of wine. She didn't really know what to expect from the DNA results. Maybe it was nothing, or perhaps it was everything she'd always wanted to know.

What she already knew was that Paul Jonas, who she'd thought was her father, didn't even exist. It was some made-up name her mother had come up with to put on the birth certificate. Someone who had been invented to satisfy her grandmother, and to blame for not stepping up, and to hang a past on. There was no Kestrel Jonas. There was a Kestrel Whoever. She didn't have her mother's last name and her alleged father, Paul Jonas, was a phantom combination of her mother's last boyfriend and the name of the doctor who delivered her.

Growing up she'd pretty much come to peace with the father who just didn't want to step up and claim her, but how did you reconcile to a person who didn't even exist?

She considered doing what Victoria had demanded. Forget the whole thing, take the money her mother offered, and stop now, before everything was destroyed. But she couldn't leave a loose end. Maybe it was all the journalism training, but she couldn't just stop.

It took some time to wend her way through the unfamiliar website and its many links, but finally, she clicked the one that said DNA Matches and waited for it to load.

A listing came up, First and foremost, initials that said full sister, G.C., and then a paternal half-brother, G.G.

Kestrel had tried to stop thinking about her father, whoever he was. All Victoria would ever say was that he was a nice man, name of Paul Jonas (printed right there on the birth certificate), and that it had just not worked out between them. She didn't know where he was and had never seen him again. He probably didn't even know about Kestrel, so it wasn't like he'd deserted her. It hadn't been a very satisfying explanation, but it was the best she could pry from Victoria's plumped lips. If she followed this Heritage thread it would never lead to a nice guy who didn't know she existed, at least not one with that name. She'd always figured that Paul Jonas had gone on his merry way and had a family somewhere, but now she knew that whoever her father was, he'd had another family somewhere as well as another child with her own mother. She couldn't really get her mind around the whole idea. There was a girl out there somewhere, identified as G.C., who was her one-hundred-percent, full-blooded sister.

Kestrel couldn't decide whether to be more furious with her mother, or more elated about her sister, or more confused about what the hell she was supposed to do about it all.

She realized that maybe she didn't want to be alone, after all. Besides, some nice aromas had escaped through Sam's door when he came out. Maybe he had enough food to share. She picked up the wine bottle and carried it and her glass onto the porch and knocked at Sam's door, careful to not spill her wine. For ordinary folks it might be a bit late to drop in, but she and Sam had agreed long ago that neither of them really led a normal life.

She could hear the TV blaring in the duplex and almost knocked a second time, thinking he might not have heard. The door swung open as she lifted her hand to the knocker. If Sam was surprised to see her, he didn't show it. He'd probably lured her over with home cooking on purpose, the whole garbage thing just a ruse to get her to come over. Was tomorrow even garbage day?

Sam's bulky frame blocked the light spilling from the kitchen but in the porch light she saw his familiar smile and the shock of unruly dark hair that spilled over his forehead. They had flirted with one another for months before her need for his professional legal help had won out over the light-hearted attraction they felt for each other. He'd planted himself in her path and she'd accidentally run into him again and again before they had both realized what they felt was fun but not serious.

"Hey."

"Hey, yourself."

"Want some wine, before it's all gone?"

"Sure, want some spaghetti, before it's all gone?"

He stepped back and she entered the duplex. The layout was the mirror image of her own, except that she had made a stab at decorating hers and he had definitely not. There was a table and two chairs for eating, a lumpy sofa, a chair for reclining, a big-screen TV for sports, and stacks of books and papers everywhere. She presumed that the bedroom contained a bed and a dresser, but she was not anxious to confirm it. Maybe a side table and lamp, since she knew there wasn't an overhead light in there.

"Sorry about the way the place looks." He looked slightly sheepish as he glanced around.

"No problem, books and papers never go out of style. Is that a new stack next to the chair?"

He looked before he realized she was joking and laughed a little.

"So, do you want some of this wine, or not?"

"Sure, sure, let me get a wineglass."

He rummaged through the cabinets looking for his non-existent wineglasses, and finally found a juice glass. She poured herself more wine. He was going to have to hurry up if he was going to get any of it to go with that spaghetti.

Kestrel was hungry. Sam was a good cook and she'd sampled his Bolognese sauce before. She was just drunk enough to think that sounded kind of risqué, and giggled.

Sam scooped a stack of books off the table and a pile of papers from a chair so that Kestrel could sit. She glanced around the room again.

"Seriously, there is even more stuff now than the last time I was here. What is all this?" She waved the hand holding her wineglass and laughed as it slopped onto the table barely missing an official-looking file folder.

"Just a project I'm working on." He dismissed the mess.

While he dished up the spaghetti and sauce and sliced some sourdough bread she looked down and nudged the pile of papers closest to the chair with her foot. Looked like legal crap. Not that it would be surprising since Sam was a lawyer, but why bring all that stuff home? Wasn't that what offices and file cabinets were for?

CHAPTER TWELVE

Saturday, June 26

When Kestrel's alarm sounded Saturday morning at five a.m. she was tempted to call in and tell her boss to go fuck himself. But she never knew when something interesting might pop up and SFUndertheRug.com had become a voracious pet that required constant feeding.

She dressed quickly in the dark and headed off to catch the early bus to Pacific Heights.

It was barely light when she keyed into the back door of the PU Club. Not many staff there at this time of day, and no members, except those who had spent the night after being over-served at dinner.

She shoved her bag into her locker and set out to find the manager for the day. She'd be setting up the breakfast buffet for the overnight guests and it served her well to be standing at the ready to observe who came down the stairs.

The past four Saturdays, Mr. Albright and Ms. Morrissey had come down the stairs together. A little too early to indicate much, but still enticing to the likes of K. Jones, or the person who used to think of herself as Kestrel Jonas, but who didn't know what to think now.

Breakfast was not a big deal on Saturday mornings. There were parties scheduled for the evening and more people, refugees from the Peninsula, would have booked rooms for the night. There was a lot to keep track of. She hadn't forgotten her contact Beatrice's revelations about the Spencer marriage and kept an eye out for signs of change. Her jaw dropped when she spied Theo Spencer coming down the broad staircase with his father's former secretary and wife-in-waiting, Rita Hawthorn. Kestrel had been getting updates from Beatrice but this was the first official sighting of the new couple. Of course, there was nothing to link the two of them, except that Ms. Hawthorn was not a member and could only have stayed as part of a member's reservation. Why were men such pricks? Rita Hawthorn had nice tits, but she was dumb as dirt and would never fit into SF society. Ducking into a corner, it took Kestrel about fifteen seconds to tweet the rare sighting with a promise of fuller details to come.

It was only the high from a good story that kept Kestrel going through her shift. Some staff might have been working in desperate need of the measly pay, but Kestrel was smiling and bowing in hopes of fucking them all over on the Internet one day. She wasn't sure when her distaste for the wealthy had begun; probably during all those years of attending schools ruled by them and waiting to get away from their influence, only to find that the big grown-up world was just high school on steroids.

After her shift ended, she had just carefully hung up her uniform jacket and pulled her purse from the locker when one of the managers, flanked by a lesser dignitary approached her.

"Ms. Jones?" His manner was official but surprisingly tentative.

"Yes?" Kestrel pulled her purse protectively to her side.

"There has been a note posted on a suspicious Internet site, Tweety, or some such thing."

"Twitter, sir." The lesser dignitary corrected.

"Ah, yes, Twitter. We have been instructed to ask each of our employees to allow us to examine their mobile phones for security."

Kestrel hesitated for only a moment before reaching into her purse and presenting her cell phone.

"Could you please activate and password the phone?" said the younger man.

"Sure." She tapped the screen and quickly thumbed in her password.

The younger man took the device and expertly scrolled through it for pictures and posts, before handing it back to her.

"Thank you, Ms. Jones. That will be all." The two men turned and left the room as Kestrel replaced the burner phone into the side pocket of her bag. The texts to her mother and cat videos had excused her from further interrogation.

Before leaving she slipped a hand into the tummy-tuck underwear that secured her real cell phone against her hip. Still there, safe and secure. Who said pantie-girdles were passé?

As she exited the building, she saw that the two managers had stopped one of her co-workers on the back stairs. She left the building with the outraged voice still ringing in her ears. "You have no right to look at my private phone."

About a block down California Street, she pulled the hidden phone from her hip and turned it back on to check messages. Two more calls from Bobby Burns, but no messages. What did he want? Annoyed, she hit call back on the phone and waited while it rang, then he answered. "Detective Burns."

"Well, hello there, Detective Burns. This is Menial Worker Jonas."

"Hey, Kestrel. I was hoping you'd call back. Wait just a second while I step outside."

As Kestrel waited at the light she glanced up and down the street. For her it paid to keep your eyes open. She'd seen more than one interesting incident on this street, although everything looked quiet today.

"Kestrel. How are you doing?"

"Fine, Bobby. Why are you calling? It's not like I've heard from you in the past six months."

"Yeah, well, this is sort of a business call."

"A business call? That doesn't sound good. Why would I have any business with the police? Aren't you in Homicide now?"

"It's just about the thing last year."

Kestrel's heart sank. "I thought that shit was over?"

"I wish." Bobby sounded sincere. "I just wanted to give you a heads up. I've been subpoenaed again, so I'm guessing you will be, too."

"Shit! What now?"

"I'm not sure, but I'm guessing that the commissioner or one of his cronies is appealing. I'll be meeting with the DA later this week."

Now, when Kestrel looked down the street, she was checking it out for a lurking process server. Sometimes they sent a policeman, but if manpower was tight, any little seedy-looking guy with shifty eyes could be the one to jump out at you from behind a garbage bin or parked car. "Okay, well thanks for the warning, though I don't know what help it is."

The silence on the other end confirmed that Bobby felt the same way. "Just letting you know."

"Okay." What else was there to say, really?

***

Bobby's partner, Detective Raquel Stafford, had watched him through the window of the coffee shop they'd been sitting in when he took the call. When he ended the call, he'd stared at the device for a long moment before slipping it into his pocket and heading back inside.

"Everything okay?" She didn't want to pry but was certainly curious.

"Yeah, everything is fine. Just some old business rearing its ugly head."

"Work business?"

"Old work business, from last year."

"Ah…" It was clear he wasn't going to elaborate, but it bothered her that his mood had changed so quickly. They'd been laughing about the lame alibi they'd heard in their last interview, and now, he really didn't look much like he wanted to laugh. She took her own phone out and scrolled through her emails while he finished his coffee, and they headed back to the station.

***

Kestrel arrived home late in the afternoon. She had put off getting there for as long as possible, stopping at Trader Joe's, and missing at least one bus on purpose.

She put her grocery bags on the porch and pulled the stack of junk mail from her mailbox, unlocked the door, and carted in her bags. As Kestrel unpacked her shopping she realized that she had not purchased anything that much resembled dinner. Wine, kiwi fruit, cheese, and marinara sauce did not sound appetizing.

The freezer was slightly more hopeful, but still required effort and imagination to become an actual meal. The cabinet mostly revealed instant oatmeal and soda crackers. Fuck, you could starve to death around here. Sam's apartment had been dark when she came home, so he wasn't going to be much help.

Finally, she snagged a sleeve of soda crackers and the peanut butter, plus a half bottle of white wine and moved to the dining room table. She'd already been concerned about her wine intake, and now she was drinking at four p.m.

Just looking at the bottle recalled the horrendous scene with Victoria just a few weeks before. Accusations, confessions, promises, she couldn't even remember who from or why. Finally, she'd left, vowing to find out the truth, whatever that was.

She waited in the dim kitchen, drinking wine, until she was sure that Sam was not going to come home to rescue her, then she typed a quick Heritage email to G.C.

CHAPTER THIRTEEN

Saturday, June 26

George found it difficult to hide his enthusiasm for today's picnic at the Bohemian Grove. Of course, he and Amélie had attended many times before, but this time he hoped it would be the last time he'd be attending as a guest. Next year he hoped to be a member in his own right.

The weather was perfect; although it was a bit foggy in San Francisco, the forecast for the North Bay looked warm and breezy. The kids were settled in with their friends and electronics and a housekeeper was on duty to assure nobody burned down the house. When they were twenty-one, they'd be able to attend and he hoped they'd enjoy it as much as he did, although they didn't show much interest now.

Gari and his wife should be there to pick them up any time, and he glanced anxiously out the front window every time he heard a car on the street. He knew it was ridiculous, but he couldn't help it.

As usual they'd been included in the luncheon being catered at Gari's camp. George kept track of who had served what to them each year so that he'd know what to serve when his turn came to host. He'd already been planning the meal.

He glanced at Amélie, sitting at the dining table reading the paper. He was so proud of her at times like this. She knew exactly what to wear for every occasion. Today her slim jeans with just the tiniest bit of bling on her well-sculpted derriere and the slightly scruffy jean jacket over a peasant top were perfect. He suspected she had paid extra to have the jacket appear well-used.

Finally, Gari's newly purchased Tesla slid silently up the driveway and, spotting it through the window, George leapt from his perch at the window. "They're here."

Amélie just shook her head. She did not understand George's excitement, and she found it surprising that he still loved the Bohemian Club trappings after so many years. She picked up her purse. "I hope you can prevent yourself from dashing down the steps and calling 'shotgun' before they even stop."

"Ha, ha, very funny." Although the long-married-couple habit of the men riding in the front and the wives in the back was well established in their foursome.

"You go ahead, I'm just going to let Linda and the kids know we are leaving and won't be back for dinner."

The comment fell flat as George had already exited the front door and was halfway down the steps.

Gari's father had been a member of the "Old Guard," those Bohemian Club members of more than forty years standing who got special seating at venues, among other privileges. George had already figured out that he'd be eighty years old before he got Old Guard designation if he got his membership this year. To him, that was one good reason to live to a ripe old age.

The drive to the twenty-seven-hundred-acre Rio Linda property of old growth redwoods took about two hours. George calculated it would take only one hour for him to drive it from the vineyard property in Sonoma when they relocated up there. Everything was working out perfectly for him.

Of course, Gari had printed their tickets and had them ready to show at the entrance to the Grove, but the pimpled kid who greeted them at the gate only asked if they were registered guests and waved them through to the nearest parking lot. George had been ready to provide the tickets and ID and was somewhat disgruntled that it seemed all you had to do to get in was pretend you were invited. He reflected that this was true of much of life and he'd bypassed many gatekeepers by assuming privilege. It was the way of the world. However, when you really did belong, it was kind of disrespectful that nobody asked.

Gari pulled into a parking spot and parked just wide of where he should have, hoping the next car would do the same. Two hundred thousand dollars for a new Tesla was nothing to sneeze at.

They boarded the transport and were dropped at the first well-stocked drink kiosk. Gin fizzes and creamy piña coladas were being dispensed at a breakneck pace and they meandered toward the first venue, drinks in hand. So many of George's friends and clients were there, it was like old home week. Not only did you get to hobnob with the rich and famous, but you were also seen to be a part of them all. Over the years more than one client had come his way from chance meetings at The Grove, even though it was strictly tabu to discuss business there.

The Bohemian Club had initially been an organization for the artists and writers, especially journalists, of San Francisco during the Gold Rush, but the money and support of the financiers and businessmen had been the life's blood of the men's club since then. U.S. presidents and world dignitaries were members and had attended the summer encampments. It was rumored that world-changing meetings had taken place here under the majestic three-hundred-foot trees.

Still, the arts were the alleged purpose behind it all and musical presentations, plays, skits, and concerts performed by the members provided the entertainment. It was considered a privilege to participate. George couldn't wait to be a part of it all.

The first performers were a quartet of *a capella* singers, followed by a comedian, and a trio of musicians.

Leaving that venue, they stopped long enough for a drink refill and a doughnut, then wandered down to the lake for a presentation about Broadway musical history by one of the members. The lake itself was steeped in custom and history, and the traditions around it made George love it even more.

It was a winding and secret path to the well-hidden camp Gari was a member of, but when they arrived the appetizers were already displayed and the bar was open. George had tried to limit his liquor consumption because when he drank too much he didn't really appreciate everything that was happening around him. He had a rosy glow at this point and sat at one of the tables feeling mellow and enjoying the activities around him. At some point Amélie had disappeared although he saw that Gari and Mary were chatting amicably with one of Gari's campmates and his guests. George could just hear the murmur of their conversation.

It looked as though lunch would be served shortly and he was trying to decide whether he wanted white wine or a beer with the porchetta and potatoes Milanese when the host, Raymond Butler, raised his voice. "I'm going to need some help bringing down some special libations from the storage shed. Who can lend me a hand?"

"Me, I'll help," George found himself saying. "I can give you a hand." He still felt pretty steady on his feet and this was an opportunity to make a good impression.

"Okay, then. Just this way." His host led the way up a rustic set of steps behind the fireplace on the edge of the patio.

They didn't go far but the path was winding and George realized that the hidden area couldn't be seen from the center of the camp.

They reached a small shed and the host threw open the door to the surprise of Amélie and George's boss, Dixon Donahue, standing in the darkened interior.

After a beat Raymond laughed. "Well, Dixon, old boy. Didn't expect you to be carrying on in the wine shed."

Amélie pulled herself together and pushed past George and down the steps. Dixon averted his eyes and spoke quickly. "Just a little business discussion. Needed a bit of privacy, is all."

"Sure, monkey business," Raymond teased. "Well, since you're here you can help us carry down these cases of Prosecco I had imported from Tuscany when I was there this spring. It will be perfect with lunch."

Dixon didn't speak but turned and hefted up one of the cases his host had gestured to.

Raymond picked up one of the cases and handed it to George. "Thanks for your help, man. I don't think I know your name."

"His name is George. George Musgrove," Dixon mumbled.

"Ah, well, thank you George. You're a good fellow."

Raymond picked up the third case and led the way down the steps followed by Dixon with George bringing up the rear.

George hadn't had that much to drink but he'd had enough to be rendered speechless by what he had seen. What had just happened? Why was Amélie in the shed with Dixon? What business did he mean?

By the time the Prosecco was delivered, ceremoniously opened, and served to a rousing toast by all in attendance, Amélie had reappeared and was standing beside George, raised glass in hand and smiling as she always was, her other hand on George's shoulder. It felt as though the little scene in the shed had never happened.

At the edge of the paved area, Raymond Butler turned to Dixon. "Where's the ex-wife? I heard she not only got half your assets, but you have to bring her to the Grove for the picnics."

"Yeah, well, she's out of town this time, thank God."

Raymond nodded toward George and Amélie. "Who's the woman?"

"George Musgrove's wife. She's the one with the money."

Raymond only nodded again and refilled his and Dixon's glasses.

George gave up his vow to limit the alcohol. After all, he wasn't driving, and the best part of the entertainment was still to come. He had several glasses of the lovely sparkling wine and allowed Amélie to guide him to the final venue where he sat in the warm sun, cooled by the breeze, and pretended he belonged here, where he wanted to be. He'd snagged a bottle of the Prosecco and carried it with him the remainder of the afternoon, until tipping the empty bottle unceremoniously into a trash bin at the edge of the parking lot. Later he would remember little of the afternoon, but he would still puzzle over the scene in the wine shed.

CHAPTER FOURTEEN

Monday, June 28

The waiter led George to a dark table toward the back of the small restaurant. Usually, he'd have refused to be seated at the table near the swinging kitchen doors and within sight of the restrooms, but tonight it was more about not being seen. He'd sent an email to Grace the previous week, pretending to be excited about finding "family" and then suggested they meet in a public place. This was perfect. It was not a dump, but not expensive. Certainly not any place his friends would see him. He sat down facing the front door and picked up the menu, immediately flipping to the wine list. He liked to think he was a connoisseur of fine wines and was a little surprised to find a couple of decent California vintages being offered. He signaled the waiter and ordered a bottle of Sauvignon Blanc and two glasses, keeping his eye on the few customers entering the place. There was almost nobody in the room at this hour and he paid little attention to the man who had walked through the door behind him and took a seat at the bar.

***

Lester Stuyvesant quickly ordered a double bourbon, not the house-brand, and settled himself in for a nice dinner. When he was on the job he read the menu from right to left, always going for the priciest entrée and augmenting it with a first course, dessert, and at least a couple of drinks. After all, he was on an expense account and it was one of the perks of his job.

It had been a cinch to follow this loser from his law office to the restaurant. He'd even parked two cars away in the parking garage. If he was cheating, he sucked at it. Lester hadn't actually met the wife, but they'd exchanged a couple of emails. She was all business and he figured this surveillance was about securing evidence rather than any emotional interest on her part. A hundred dollars an hour and expenses. Perfect for him. He'd done a number of jobs for George's firm but had never followed one of the attorneys before.

He was between acting roles and liked these private dick gigs because he figured they let him practice his acting skills. He thought he knew how to dress and act so that this guy wouldn't even notice him there, watching everything that went on.

He might have been a bit more obvious than he thought he was. His recent obsession with Tyrion Lannister and "Game of Thrones" had caused his usually drab wardrobe to be kicked up by unusual flourishes like leather vests, longer hair, and a bit more facial hair than usual. Lester was not tall, though not an actual "little person." Until recently he'd been a fan of higher-heeled boots, hats, and elongating lines. Now he leaned more in the direction of making himself more distinctively short. He had added a bit of swagger to his walk, though he lacked Tyrion's presence, and he had almost mastered scrambling up onto tall barstools without drawing attention to himself. His technique included gripping the edge of the bar and making a quick step onto the lower railing. He usually frequented bars where the stools were not too high, the railing was not too slippery, and he could get good leverage on the way on and off. This restaurant was so-so but you couldn't always pick where you wanted to drink. He'd found that most romantic trysts were not conducted at the higher-end places. It was an art, choosing a decent place to impress the girlfriend without exposing yourself to unexpected encounters with the wife's friends.

Lester had just ordered a second drink and George was halfway through his first glass of wine, when a young woman entered the restaurant. She glanced around tentatively but George stood quickly and raised his arm so she would see him right away. Grace had told George she'd be wearing a red sweater and boots, and she looked about the right age.

She smiled at George and walked quickly to the table. If Lester had been expecting them to embrace, he was a little surprised by the handshake that passed between the two. They sat and she laughed nervously at something George said.

***

George poured a glass of wine for Grace and watched her as she studied the menu. Not his type, but nice-looking. She seemed familiar though he could not have said where he had ever seen her. Glossy mid-length hair, with those expensive highlights his wife and her friends loved so much. Clear skin, little makeup. Nicely dressed, but not flashy. He wouldn't mind having her as a sister. She looked a lot nicer than George's wife's sister, Bridget. When the waiter came, she put down her menu and ordered confidently. George ordered the special, whatever that was, and poured himself some more wine.

***

Grace was excited to meet this man she thought was her brother. He didn't look much like her, with his dark hair and eyes and he was probably only an inch or so taller than she was. But then, she didn't know if she resembled her mother or her father, so there was no surprise there. He looked like a professional guy: clean-shaven, nice suit and tie, maybe moving a little toward pudgy, but not fat. He acted like he was happy she was there, although he did glance furtively toward the door each time it opened.

They exchanged the small-talk sort of pleasantries that are usual between strangers and fell silent when their food arrived. Grace hadn't realized how hard it would to be to raise the questions she had; twenty-eight years of questions. She wasn't quite sure regarding the etiquette of grilling someone about his, and your own, existence. Miss Manners had never mentioned that in any of her columns.

***

Lester was thoroughly enjoying his dinner but was mystified by the couple he observed in the mirror behind the bar. If this was a rendezvous, it was the weirdest one he'd ever seen. The wife might be expecting to find a girlfriend, but this looked more like an interview for an intern at the guy's office. He wished he'd opted for a table closer to the action, although there didn't seem to be much conversation going on.

The couple had finished dinner and the woman held her glass out to George. He poured them both the last of the bottle and signaled the waiter to bring another.

***

George was surprised he was finding it so hard to broach the subject of Grace's relationship to Gari's family. Usually, he could bullshit with the best of them. It had gotten him through law school and married into the best family, but now he felt stymied by Grace's vulnerability. In a way, it pissed him off. Foremost on his mind was the money that he was expecting from Garrett Graham's estate, and the cash Gari would be gathering for him. One hundred thousand in tidy bundles of hundred-dollar bills. He'd hoped that Grace would turn out to be what he'd expected to find: an ill-educated, average girl with a nowhere job who'd be thrilled to receive a few thousand dollars, hell, maybe even fifty thousand, in compensation for being given up for adoption. Instead, here she was: intelligent, confident, capable, and just a little shy over the whole thing.

Suddenly, Grace seemed to make a decision. She leaned forward and moved the chair closer to the table. She swallowed the last of her wine, and gazing at George, she asked, "What is our father like?"

"Our, um, father is, was, a good guy: Successful, good-looking, a pretty good guy."

"Was? Does that mean he died?"

"Yes, God, I'm sorry, I keep forgetting you don't really know anything about him."

She sat back in her chair. "I was hoping I had found him, and it turns out I am too late." She looked stricken.

"Well, he was pretty old, you know. In his seventies. It was last year and happened pretty fast. Not a lot of suffering..."

"That's good, I guess. I just hoped I would have a chance to get to meet him, to know him a little, to know about my mother."

George said nothing. The waiter had delivered the freshly opened wine bottle, so he quickly poured himself a glass.

Grace picked up her glass and held it out for a refill.

"What was his name?"

Oddly, George had not been ready for that question. He'd given her a fake name himself and realized he'd not thought to make up one for their alleged father. He'd stuck with his own first name and added the surname Gregory, easy to remember. George Gregory to match the Heritage initials of G.G. So, the obvious thing was to make his dad Garrett Gregory.

"Garrett Gregory," Grace seemed to swish the name around in her mouth like she was tasting her wine. At least she swallowed instead of spitting it out.

"What is your mother's name?" Another question George was not prepared for.

"Um, Trudy. Actually, Gertrude but she hated that name." What was it they said about lying? Make the lie as truthful as possible so you had less to remember. His mother did hate the name Gertrude. At least they hadn't called her Gertie, for short.

"Do you have brothers and sisters, George?"

"Yes, I have two younger sisters." Gari did have two sisters, although George did not. This was starting to get complicated. He hoped this would be the only conversation they would have and he wouldn't have to keep the lies straight.

"Have you told them about me?"

"Not really." He saw the disappointment on her face. "Not yet. I wanted to meet you first. It will be kind of a shock, you know."

Grace laughed, "I guess it will. It was a shock for me, but probably not as much. I'm anxious to meet them; I've never had any siblings. Is your mother still alive?

"No, she died a few years ago, cancer."

Shit, George could see he was getting in over his head. How did he offer her money to go away? He couldn't introduce Gari and the girls. There was never going to be some big family reunion: no Easter brunches, no July potlucks, no caroling around the Christmas tree.

He decided to make one stab at Plan A, buying her off, but his head was reeling from that last glass of wine. Grace's face looked flushed as well.

"Listen, Grace, I know my dad must have felt really badly about you, if he even knew. I mean, DNA doesn't lie, but maybe your mother never even told him. Maybe it was a one-night stand, or something."

The look on Grace's face told him he probably was getting off on the wrong track. "Never mind, that's not what I meant. Just, Dad never mentioned it, and he wasn't that kind of guy."

Grace just stared at him.

"My sisters are going to be upset about this. Everything about who their dad, our dad, was will be different. How do you explain it to the kids?"

"I don't know how you explain it to the kids. Maybe the way my adoptive parents explained it to me."

"I mean, there was a trust when he died. I could arrange for you to get some of the money."

"And what, just disappear into the woodwork, again?"

Even in his inebriated state George could see this wasn't going well. He'd have to revert to Plan B, whatever that was. For now, he needed to get out of here and clear his head.

"Never mind, I was just blathering. Too much wine. Let me talk to my sisters and get back in touch with you next week."

Grace had gone very quiet, but she seemed to be thinking it over. There was a hint of skepticism in the look she gave him, but she knew how to reach him if he didn't get in touch. It was right there on Heritage.com, right there in the email he'd sent her.

"Look, Grace, it's dark out there and starting to get cold. Let me drive you home and we'll talk next week."

"Okay." She stood unsteadily. "I just live a few blocks from here."

George had already paid the check with cash and took her elbow to steer her down the street to the parking garage.

Neither of them noticed Lester Stuyvesant slip out of the restaurant behind them and follow them to the car.

Grace directed George to the condo complex on Fulton Street and he idled the car at the curb as he watched her walk up the stairs and unlock the door to her place. He was watching her but he felt like he was watching a huge chunk of the Graham fortune walk out of his life. He'd already been spending that money in his daydreams. What was he going to tell Gari? He hadn't solved the problem; he'd probably made it worse.

Lester's car idled about half a block back and he shook his head as he watched Grace get out alone and weave her way to her front door.

When George pulled out Lester did, as well, and followed him through the drizzly San Francisco traffic to the house in Pacific Heights. Weirdest date he'd ever seen, but he'd get paid no matter how weird it was.

***

Grace leaned back against the closed door. The streetlights shone through the window illuminating the small living room.

How could you be so disappointed by something you had no expectations of? She hadn't expected affection or an overflow of love on seeing him, but maybe she'd thought there would be some warmth, some welcome.

She took a bottle of sparkling water from the fridge and sat down at the table in front of her laptop. Maybe now was not the best time for her to analyze the evening, still feeling a little woozy from the wine. The cold water cleared away some of the mucky taste in her mouth.

The laptop lit up as she touched the screen. She had intended to go to bed, but the smiling little email icon was irresistible.

Subject line: You Don't Know Me, I think I'm Your Sister.

Grace gazed at the screen for a few seconds then reached out and shut it down. Enough. She turned out the light and walked slowly into the bedroom. She fell into bed fully clothed. As she dozed off she thought of the one other time in her life when she'd done that. She had been stoned then, but tonight she was just deflated.

CHAPTER FIFTEEN

Monday, June 28

It was late enough that George's drive home took just a few minutes. He pulled into the garage and the door slid closed behind him. The fog had drifted in off the bay and George took a moment to be glad for the private parking. He could recall the days of driving in circles looking to park near his apartment and walking home in the chill air. But gratitude had its limits and what he most wanted was a stiff drink and the comfort of his study. Before that he would have to make it through the gauntlet of the family waiting upstairs.

Actually, the kids would have already retreated to their rooms with their phones and game consoles and it would just be Amélie waiting for him. That was daunting enough.

He climbed the stairs to the main floor of the house. Across the formal entry he could see that a fire blazed in the fireplace. Some classical music played in the background. He didn't see Amélie and wondered whether it was possible to get from the door to the bar to his study without running into her.

"Well, at last you're home." No such luck.

He turned to his wife with a brittle smile. "I told you I had a client dinner. It's not late you know."

Amélie shrugged and turned toward the living room.

Damn, he'd have to talk to her while she poured him two fingers of Chivas Regal 25. "So, how was your day?"

***

Amélie placed her wineglass on the bar and poured his scotch into a heavy crystal glass. She didn't relish talking to him, either but she'd promised Dixon she'd do it tonight. Before George had arrived, she'd received a text from Lester Stuyvesant, the PI, letting her know that George had arrived and Lester was clocking out. "More to follow," it had said. Whatever that meant.

She smiled and handed him the glass. "It was fine, no surprises." It seemed funny to her that there had been a day when she'd have been waiting anxiously for George to come home. They'd have kissed lightly and laughed over dinner and wine. They'd have watched TV in front of the fire or gone upstairs to spend some time with the kids. Had all of that been a lie? She thought now that George had little love for her. For a long time she'd thought there was at least affection, but now she wasn't so sure. George seemed headed for his study so she quickly stepped between him and the door.

"Can we talk for a few minutes?"

Her tone told George that it was no good to claim exhaustion or work to complete, so he turned back and sat down on one end of the sofa. Amélie perched across from him on the edge of her chair. She fiddled nervously with her wineglass and hesitated.

"Look, can we do this later? I've had a rough day." There was still a chance that George could make a run for the end zone.

"No, I need to talk to you now. I think you should move out, George. You've already checked out of my life, and I want you out of my house."

***

He noted the "my house" reference and his first reaction was anger. He took a deep breath because he knew only too well what a separation or divorce would mean for his lifestyle. God knew he could live without the family and the hassles, but he had no intention of living without the perks of real wealth. He would need to do some serious groveling.

"Amélie, honey, you can't mean that." He set his glass on the marble tabletop, remembering to use the required coaster, and stood. "I love you and the kids. You can't expect me to let you go." He stepped toward her but hesitated as she recoiled from him. Still, he reached out and took her arm, drawing her to him. She turned her head away but did not withdraw. His arms slid around her and he began to sway with the strains of the waltz playing on KDFC.

When the music ended, he held her and waited to speak until he felt her rigid body begin to relax and lean into him a bit.

"Baby, I know I've not been here for you lately. I just feel like you and the kids don't need me anymore." That was good, make it her fault they'd grown apart.

***

Amélie had forgotten how gentle he could be, how persuasive. She suspected it was bullshit, but she wanted him to care about her. Wanted to keep her marriage whole. Hated the idea of admitting to the world that her family wasn't perfect. What was it Dixon had said? "He doesn't deserve you. He doesn't know what he has. He knows the cost of everything and the value of nothing."

***

"I don't deserve you," he whispered in her ear.

She wasn't quick to contradict him, and that threw him for a minute. He was in deeper shit than he'd thought.

"Can't we sleep on it and talk in the morning?" If he could get her into bed he'd be able to distract her. He wasn't a bad lover when he bothered to make the effort.

George picked up her glass and the bottle of wine. At the bottom of the stairs, he put them down, then drew her to him and kissed her, at first gently and then more deeply.

Amélie knew that Dixon would be mad tomorrow, but there was no harm in one more night together. Maybe they could still work this out.

George did not know about Dixon, but he knew his time was short. He'd have very little time to come up with a plan.

CHAPTER SIXTEEN

Tuesday, June 29

George woke in a foul temper, but with the beginnings of a plan. He'd be damned if either Amélie or Grace would keep him from coming out on top. He didn't see his wife before he left for the office. This was one of the days she helped at the kids' school. George couldn't imagine what she could do that would be of any benefit to any of those rich brats. Maybe she gave classes in walking with a stick up her ass. Who knew?

He was having lunch with Gari today, so he called Gari's private office line as soon as he reached the office. "Gari, hey, it's George. Good news for both of us. That sister of yours is sleazy and jumped at the chance to slide on out of your life for a little filthy lucre. Sorry, she wouldn't go for anything less than the hundred thousand and she wants it ASAP. I think she's planning on quitting her loser job and heading for Mexico first thing. Give me a call and let me know when you can get the money together. I'll see you at lunch."

Gari never got into the office early, but he must have checked the messages from home because he called George back within half an hour.

George thought Gari must really be anxious to get this over with, because he didn't even ask any questions, and, miracle of miracles, he had spent the last few days pulling chunks of money out of different accounts in case he needed it. He had gotten his hands on sixty thousand dollars, but it would take him another week to get the rest.

George was elated, "No problem, I can probably stall her for a few days if I get her the first half. Can you bring the cash to the club at lunch?"

"Sure, I guess. It's in the safe at the office. I'll bring it with me."

***

Amélie was surprised to get a call from George before lunchtime. She was just leaving the school to meet an old college friend for lunch. She was even more surprised that he remembered her friend, Manon, was in town for a few days. She'd been sure he hadn't been listening when she'd mentioned the visit to him the week before. When George proposed that they take Manon with them to the opera on Thursday, he brushed off her questions about getting another ticket. "Not a problem. I can just get a single for myself for Thursday and Manon can have my seat." Amélie would have asked more questions if she hadn't been so shocked. George's favorite thing about the freaking opera season tickets was sitting where everyone could see him and he could impress all the surrounding seat holders with his vast knowledge of opera. Giving up his seat up for one of Amélie's "stuck-up" classmates was the last thing she expected, but she wasn't going to argue with him about it.

"Wow, George, what a great idea. I'm just leaving to meet Manon for lunch and I can tell her then."

"Do you two want to have lunch at the PU Club? I'm meeting Gari there myself today."

"Um, no, we're going to Macy's so we can get some shopping done."

***

George had counted on her declining to meet him for lunch. You can't very well trash your husband to your oldest friend if he's sitting right there. Plus, he got a couple of extra brownie points for even suggesting having lunch together. The reason he wanted to invite her, and the reason she would never come, was because she had to be invited by Gari and couldn't eat in the main dining room at the PU Club. It chafed her butt and he knew it. One point for George, zero for Amélie.

The final call before leaving for lunch was to the opera house box office to secure the promised single ticket for Thursday night. He picked the one farthest from where he usually sat and went cheap. He wasn't going to actually watch the opera, so it didn't matter where he sat.

The weather in SF was fine for this time of year and George left early for lunch and walked to the PU Club. He loved being seen at the front entrance, and once again loitered until the cable car was unloading its flock of gawking tourists before entering the building. What was the point in belonging if nobody envied you? Of course, they didn't see him duck around the side of the building and in the back door where non-members were required to check in.

Gari waved at him the second he strode into the main dining room. There were already glasses of wine poured and George immediately noted the briefcase at Gari's feet. George didn't know Gari even owned a briefcase.

"I'm glad you're on time. I'm kind of rushed today." Gari looked flushed and his eyes glittered oddly.

"You have time for lunch though, right?"

"Sure, but I want to get back to the office. I'm meeting with one of the attorneys about the trust."

George picked up the menu. Good, crab cakes, one of his favorites. Crab, a nice white wine, and sixty thousand dollars. It was going to be a great afternoon.

After they had ordered, Gari slid the briefcase from one side of his chair to the space between them. They ate in silence, Gari anxious to leave, and when they stood up and walked away, the lovely case of money went with George.

It was a nice case, probably worth at least five hundred dollars. One more thing to add to the asset list.

George would have liked to linger, have another glass of wine, maybe some dessert. Nah, he didn't need it, that expensive suit of his was getting a bit snug. He'd head back to the office, slide the money into his hidden cache, and go home early. Maybe he'd order another couple of nice suits before Amélie decided to cut off the credit account at Brooks Brothers.

CHAPTER SEVENTEEN

Tuesday, June 29

Grace had not visited the California Academy of Sciences since her parents took her there as a child. It had been remodeled and she felt a surprising excitement. She had dressed carefully for this visit. Kind of dressy, she guessed, but it seemed a sign of respect for the occasion to wear a skirt and kitten heels. Her sleek hair gleamed in the sunshine as she ascended the steps, taking in all the new sights. The entrance by the dinosaur skeleton was where she'd arranged to meet her sister. It felt strange to think those words, and she was cautious about expectations since her uncomfortable meeting with George. She had chosen the place so that her time wouldn't be wasted if the meeting were a bust. At least she'd be able to check out the exhibits and get a bite of lunch even if Kestrel didn't show up, which seemed possible since it was already fifteen minutes past the designated hour.

***

At that moment, she was almost within touching distance of Kestrel, and was being carefully checked out by her younger sibling. Unlike Grace, Kestrel had dressed down for the meeting. She'd taken the bus over and worn her usual invisible outfit. However, she'd brought a sports bag containing a change of clothes and some emergency makeup.

Kestrel had spotted Grace coming up the steps. It was strange to recognize someone you'd never met, but not surprising that they would look similar. She'd ducked into the restroom and done a quick change. Emerging looking a little more respectable, she'd still hung back, lurking behind an inadequate pillar. She was angry with herself for feeling so nervous. That person over there by the dinosaur, the one who looked like the Neiman-Marcus version of herself, had never been in her life before, and would leave no hole if they never met. Except that wasn't true. Kestrel was drawn to her with a palpable yearning, but still held back. She sensed that Grace, having purchased her admission, was set to give up on their meeting and head for the entrance to the first exhibit. Finally, she stepped forward and tentatively spoke her name, above a whisper, but not much. "Grace."

***

Grace started and turned quickly.

It was like gazing into a foggy mirror and for a few seconds they just stared, then Grace laughed nervously. "Kestrel… I suppose I should have known we'd look alike, but I didn't realize how much." Blue eyes that matched her own gazed back. Grace was a little taller, or maybe she stood straighter than Kestrel. Her hair was salon-highlighted while Kestrel's heightened blond came from a box and her darker roots had begun to show. The advantages of braces, facials, and well-used gym memberships showed on Grace. Kestrel reached her hand out and Grace stepped forward and threw her arms around her sister.

"I knew you would come. I am so happy to meet you," Grace said.

For once Kestrel didn't have any idea what she should say or do. When Grace stepped back she took hold of Kestrel's hand. "Let's look around. I bought both of us tickets. I knew you would come." Grace turned and led her toward the entrance and Kestrel followed, the older sister leading the younger.

They wandered through the exhibits, still holding hands. Grace had not tried to draw away and Kestrel had held on. Every so often Grace would comment on one of the exhibits, but Kestrel rarely replied. She really didn't even hear what Grace said; she just drank her in.

"Have you been here since the remodel?" Kestrel realized that Grace has spoken directly to her.

"No, I haven't been here since I was a kid."

"Me either. Funny, I moved to San Francisco to be close to all these places, but I hardly ever find time to go to them. I live three blocks from the opera house and I have never gone to an opera."

Kestrel grimaced. "Me either, thank God." They both laughed.

Kestrel had finally loosened her grip on Grace and followed her through the next exhibit. She had begun to feel safe in looking away, that the chimera would not disappear. Still, she didn't stray very far.

It was good that there were so many things to look at here as neither of them had the slightest idea what to say. Grace had set the gentle pace and Kestrel was happy to follow along. They had come to the café and Grace realized her stomach was rumbling. "Let's get something to eat. Is here okay?"

Kestrel picked up one of the menus at the entrance and was relieved to see burgers and pizza. Too often San Francisco eateries gave her little to choose from, primarily vegan or vegetarian options with a little gluten-free thrown in for good measure.

"Sure, this would be fine." She glanced up at the wall clock and realized that she needed to leave if she was going to make her evening shift at The Towers. "Find a table while I make a quick phone call, okay?" There was no way she was going to leave right now. Of course, her manager at The Towers acted as though the world would come to an untimely and calamitous end because she didn't come to work. She coughed and gagged enough to convince him that he was saving the lives of many of the elderly residents by letting her beg off. In fact, she noted at least two of the café patrons who'd overheard her call took distant seats when she followed Grace to the table by the window.

It didn't surprise her that Grace ordered the organic chicken salad wrap while Kestrel was trying to decide between the pulled pork sandwich or the tuna melt and bemoaning the unavailability of fries.

"If we were from out of town, we'd be required to order the clam chowder in a bread bowl, I think," Grace joked after they had placed their orders.

After several futile attempts at small talk, Kestrel gave up and went to the counter, returning with two double white wines.

"I hope you drink wine. Otherwise, I'll have to assume Heritage hooked me up with the wrong sister."

"Oh no, I love my wine." Grace reached out for the glass and Kestrel felt as though she was smiling at herself. Maybe for the first time in her life.

Their lunches came and the wine kicked in. They talked about Palo Alto. Kestrel had spent months at a time there with her grandmother, going to Palo Alto High School, just down the street from Grace's private school.

"You know what we used to say about Castilleja girls, don't you?"

"No, but if it had to do with being snotty and slutty it was probably right. We weren't very complimentary about Paly girls ourselves."

"Really, what did you say?"

"You mean other than making fun of your taste in clothes and lack of appreciation for being surrounded by all that testosterone?"

"I always thought going to a girls' school might help on concentration."

"Maybe if you weren't worrying about the "mean girls" surrounding you."

Kestrel stood up to get more wine but Grace touched her arm. "Let's Uber to my condo. I've got wine and snacks."

When their ride came, an early-balding guy in a Kia, he hopped out to open the door for Grace, looking her over appreciatively.

"So, are you two twins?" The suggestive note in his voice prompted a smirk from Kestrel.

"No, just sisters, so you can stuff your fantasies."

He raised both palms in denial.

"No, no, just curious."

The music on the radio changed as they pulled from the curb and the jangling strains of a Middle Eastern dance tune came on.

"I know this tune, Mom used to belly dance and this was part of her music." Kestrel laughed and made finger-cymbal motions with her thumbs and middle fingers.

"Our mom was a belly dancer?" Grace's eyes grew wide.

"Among other things, she loved that kind of stuff."

Grace paused. "I cannot even begin to imagine Madeleine, my adopted mom, doing such a thing."

"Well, I can't imagine our mom, Victoria, not doing it."

"You have got to tell me all about her."

"I will, but not all at one time, it would blow your mind."

During the drive Grace and Kestrel whispered to one another, sneaking looks at the back of the driver's head.

"He's not bad."

"Well, I'd do him in a pinch."

"What do you mean?" Grace pulled back and looked shocked. "What makes you think he'd choose you?"

They both dissolved in giggles just as they pulled up in front of the condo.

The driver did not get out to open the door for Grace. Although you weren't supposed to tip Uber drivers, Grace leaned over the front seat and slipped a twenty-dollar bill into his hand.

They helped each other navigate up the stairs and Kestrel waved at the passing tour bus of gawkers while Grace rummaged through her purse for the key.

"I have to pee or I'll wet my pants," gasped Grace as she headed for the bathroom. The condo was small; it could almost all be seen from the front door. The standard one-plus bedroom. Kestrel shrugged off her jacket and turned in a circle taking in Grace's personal space. Not bad. Neat as a pin, and Pottery Barn chic, right down to the colors of the year. She walked to the bookshelf with its array of family photos. Grace and her adopted parents, Kestrel guessed, Grace at different ages and places: Disneyland, Hawaii, Grand Canyon, Stanford graduation, and a photo of her with a good-looking metro-sexual on a well-maintained ski slope. Kestrel thought he looked familiar but was distracted by Grace emerging from the bathroom tugging her skirt down over her thighs.

"My turn." Kestrel entered the sparkling bath. Huh, Grace must have gotten the obsessive-compulsive gene.

She flushed the toilet and ran the water to cover the sound of opening the medicine cabinet. Advil, birth control pills, toothpaste. Boring. Not even any anti-fungal creams or antibiotics.

Grace had already poured wine into glasses and put out a basket of gluten-free crackers. "I've got brie and Velveeta," she said.

"Hell, bring it all. I've got cannabis mints and dark chocolate in the bottom of this bag." Kestrel flopped on the prettily tufted sofa. "So, who's the dude with the million-dollar smile and the dimples in the picture there?"

Grace waved dismissively at the photo shelf. "Just a guy. His grandma and my folks are hopeful, but he's kind of an asshole."

"Aren't they all?"

"So far, yeah. This guy's pretty into himself though, and I still haven't figured out where I fit in the picture."

Kestrel could feel Grace's reticence about discussing the boyfriend, so she dropped the subject. There would be plenty of time to hash over relationships.

The topics ranged wide, although neither of them remembered much of it the next day. What Kestrel did remember was Grace's tearful description of her meeting with their half-brother. Kestrel admitted that she had feared that her meeting with Grace would be like that, and then they both cracked up at Grace's description of the brother and his awkward attempt at buying her off.

Grace sighed, "I'd hoped I'd see something of me in him, but he just looked like he wished I hadn't shown up, or that I would go away easily. I thought he might want me to meet the family and at least get to know me, but him offering me money just set the wrong tone."

"Maybe I can get him to offer me some money." Kestrel looked hopeful.

"You're going to take me to meet our mom, right?"

For a moment Kestrel was stunned. For some reason it had not occurred to her that she, Victoria, and Grace could be in the same space at the same time. "Sure, but not too soon, I don't want to scare you off. Are you going to try to see him again? Maybe I could go along and really blow his mind."

"I don't really want to see him, but he said he'd bring some pictures of our dad and sisters. I'd like to see those."

"Yeah, well let me know and we'll get together and punk him."

At some point they had both fallen asleep sprawled across the sofa, but Kestrel started awake at five-fifteen. "Holy shit, I have to work this morning."

"Yeah, me too. What time is it?"

"Almost daylight."

Kestrel stood up and sat back down, clutching her head.

"Are you okay?" Grace did not even try to stand.

"Yeah, I am an expert at working while still stoned. But I do have to get home and change before work." She disappeared into the bathroom with her purse and emerged, hair combed and face washed in about two minutes.

"Well, thanks for everything. Best slumber party ever." Kestrel started to shake Grace's hand but Grace grabbed her and gave her a quick hug.

"I think we're past shaking hands. I want to make this a weekly event."

Kestrel hugged back and then let herself out the door. Grace watched her down the stairs and as she disappeared down the street toward Civic Center.

Closing the door, she began dreaming up a good excuse to leave her boss for why she wouldn't be in today and headed toward her beckoning bedroom.

Kestrel hunched her shoulders in the damp morning fog, or as it was better known locally, the marine layer. Two bus rides and a brisk walk got her home as the day brightened.

She ran through the shower, pulled on the PU Club uniform, brushed her teeth, and pulled her wet hair back into a long tail on her way out the door.

"Fifteen minutes, damn I'm good." Her head was clearing from the long night, and she was buoyed with a surprising joy she couldn't remember often feeling in her life. Things were looking up, though she didn't have a clue what to do next. For today, it felt good to know she had a sister in the world.

CHAPTER EIGHTEEN

Thursday, July 1

Morning was never good for Kestrel. She'd guess she was a night owl if she cared enough to guess. That morning she couldn't convince herself to open her eyes, much less get up and face the day. It was working two shifts yesterday after the late night with Grace, she told herself, but she knew it was really that she would no longer recognize the world out there. She had always known her mother had a sketchy relationship with the truth, depending on whether it benefited her, but Kestrel had convinced herself that her mother just didn't like reality all that much. Sometimes the lies were to Kestrel, but usually they were to other people and Kestrel felt no responsibility for setting things straight.

She had been happy to find her sister, but now her previous life felt like a lie: a needless, selfish, endless, convoluted, fucking, pile-of-shit lie. No wonder Victoria had gone bonkers when she heard about Heritage. Kestrel didn't want to think about her mother, or see her, or talk to her, but she couldn't un-know these new truths. She had to get a straight answer from Victoria, and in her experience, that was not an easy thing to do.

Finally, she got up. She had a lunch shift at the PU Club, but she called in sick. At first Casper, her manager, didn't understand what she was telling him. Miss Jones had never missed a shift or even been late. He'd been counting on her to pick up the slack from the two new staffers starting today. Eventually, he accepted the inevitable and turned his mind to how he could cover everything, but not before grudgingly telling Miss Jones to "get well soon."

"Yeah, well, fuck you, too," she thought as she hung up the phone.

As she drove across the Golden Gate Bridge she tried to focus on the sunny skies, the skittering sailboats, the mass of amazed tourists making their way across the span. She hoped Victoria would be home. It was a Thursday and sometime in Victoria's youth, a fortune teller had told her that it was unlucky to run errands on Thursdays. So, unless she was traveling, she was usually home on that day. Kestrel had thought about calling ahead but didn't want to give her mother a chance to beg off. Victoria didn't like drop-in visitors; she said it threw her off-kilter. That was exactly what Kestrel wanted. An on-kilter Victoria was cagey prey.

She parked her car in the well-hidden space behind the hedge. There was no answer to her knock, so she let herself in. Walking through the sunny rooms, she thought how much of her mother was expressed in the décor. Everything was white and pale blue. The shelves were full of mementos from her travels (no family snapshots or clay handprints here). The walls were crowded with paintings left behind by Grandma McKenzie, and Victoria's own poster-sized, free-style art. Not surprisingly, she found her mother in the hot tub on the deck. It was one of Victoria's favorite places to relax. The view of San Francisco and the Bay was breathtaking. It was also not surprising that Victoria was naked. She loved her body and worked at keeping it up. She was lovely for fifty-four years old, looked forty-four, and usually dressed like she was twenty-four. Her blond hair was long and piled loosely on top of her head, restrained by a scrunchy.

Victoria was not happy to see Kestrel. She'd spent a lot of time since their last encounter wondering how bad this was going to get and how to get out of it. It was too bad that Kestrel knew her so well; the usual dodges and dances wouldn't work very well.

"I wasn't expecting anyone today."

"Well, I wasn't expecting to need to be here today, Mom."

"While you're standing there, could you hand me my towel?"

"Sure. Are you going to get out, or do you want to talk here?" Kestrel held out the towel.

Victoria seemed to consider whether there was another option to the talk part of the question, but finally took the towel and stepped out of the tub. Wrapping herself in the towel she strode into the house as regally as possible.

She didn't bother getting dressed. Kestrel sensed that her mother thought that facing her naked in her own space would sway the conversation to her benefit. Kestrel was over the mind games and prevarication. She was not leaving this house today without an understanding of what the hell had happened to her life.

"It's a little early for wine. Why don't you make a pot of coffee?"

"Sure, Victoria, I can do that."

"So, you're calling me Victoria today instead of Mom. You must be annoyed about something."

Kestrel filled the coffee carafe and carefully poured water into the maker. "Yeah, you might say that."

Victoria sighed. "What is it now? Aren't you getting a little old for hashing over the old grudges?"

Kestrel pushed the on-button on the coffeemaker. "Yeah, if this was an old grudge, but this is a completely new grudge. Why didn't you tell me you had another daughter you gave up for adoption before I was born?" There, it was out there, and she thought Victoria paled a bit as she widened her big brown eyes. Kestrel was used to that old trick, as well. Looking all "deer in headlights" while you tried to come up with a good story.

"Because it wasn't any of your business. I don't know anything about that baby. I never asked."

"Well, I do know a lot about her. Her name is Grace, she looks a lot like me, and, no thanks to you, she's had a fabulous life."

"Well, if that's the case, then it is all due to me. Your sister had a good life, so why bring all of this up?"

"Because, Victoria, she also had the same father I had. How can that be?"

Victoria turned away. She may not have stamped her little foot, but she was mentally doing it. "What does that have to do with anything? You don't know him. She doesn't know him. What difference does it make?"

"The difference is that it makes every fucking thing you ever told me a big fat lie."

"Language, Kestrel. You don't have to be so crude. Besides, I wasn't lying to you; it just didn't matter who your father was. I didn't want to talk about it then, and I don't want to talk about it now."

Victoria looked as though she would sweep out the room in high dudgeon, except that Kestrel stepped between her and the nearest door.

"If you don't mind, I want to get dressed. It's cold in here."

"Sure, but I am coming in with you. There aren't going to be any more closed doors."

Victoria huffed into the bedroom and snagged a silky robe off the hook on the door.

"Fine, what is it you want to know?"

"I want to know who my father was. How long were you together, why did you give Grace up for adoption, and why the hell did you keep me?"

Kestrel followed Victoria back into the kitchen and watched her pour two cups of coffee. After she had fiddled with the cups for a few minutes and wiped the counter off three times, Victoria sat down at the table.

Kestrel dropped into the other chair slopping her coffee onto her jeans, but she didn't really notice.

"I was young and struggling as a photographer. He was married and had kids. When I got pregnant the first time, I waited too long to get an abortion. I kept thinking he'd leave his wife and marry me, but that didn't happen."

Victoria gazed out the window for several seconds. Kestrel finally started to speak but Victoria interrupted her.

"He had money and he helped me out a lot, and I was stupid enough to think he really cared about anyone but himself. When I got pregnant with you, he was furious. He demanded that I have an abortion. That's when I really knew that he cared nothing about me, and I told him I was going to have the baby and keep it…you."

"Why? Why would you keep me?"

Another sigh, "There were a lot of reasons. Most of them sound pretty lame now. I thought I loved him and wanted to keep his child, I still hoped he'd change his mind, I wanted to have a hold on him, I guess."

"Did you keep fucking him? Did he give you money?"

"No, I didn't keep fucking him, as you so nicely put it. He didn't want anything to do with either of us. And, yes, he did give me money when I needed it."

Kestrel stood up so suddenly that her chair slid back and crashed to the floor. She placed both hands on the table and leaned very close to her mother's face. "You used me to get money from him? I was a bargaining chip for you!"

Victoria stood up as well. "That's not true. I thought I could be a good mother to you, that someone in the world would have to love me."

"Well, you were wrong on both counts then, weren't you?"

Their voices had risen, and Victoria burst into tears. "That's a terrible thing to say. I've done the best I could for you. I didn't know it would be so *hard*." Her voice quavered on the last word.

"I can't believe this. Who was this guy? Grace says he's dead, but what was his name?"

"I'm not going to tell you his name. It's none of your business. How does she know he's dead? Who's she been talking to?"

"She's met his son, the asshole, and he told her his father was dead. But you already knew that didn't you? The payments must have stopped."

"There weren't payments. He just helped me when I asked him. I signed a paper saying that I'd never tell you his name, that was part of the deal."

"Well, I guess 'the deal' didn't take DNA into account, because now it is all out there. No more dirty little secrets."

Kestrel could tell by her mother's expression that the conversation was about to be over. There was a point when she could see Victoria shutting down and Kestrel had seen it many times in her life. A calmness would set in and there would be no point in talking, and Kestrel didn't really think she could handle the shutdown. She would want to shake her mother until her teeth rattled in her head, but there would be no use. She grabbed the purse she had left next to the coffeemaker and walked out the kitchen door. She gave the door an extra-hard slam and looked up to see the neighbor peering over the hedge to see what all the racket was about. She smiled and waved and the head ducked out of sight.

Getting in her car, she started the engine and let it idle for a few minutes, hoping her mother would come out to bring her back, but knowing that was not going to happen. Kestrel was sure that Victoria had sighed in relief when she left. Her mother could put everything off to another day. Any other day. But, for now, all would be well. She'd turn off her phone and get back in the hot tub. Maybe she'd open some wine or have just a bite of the frozen Key lime pie she kept for just such emergencies. She would hear the roar of the little VW engine spattering gravel up the driveway and turn her mind to other things.

CHAPTER NINETEEN

Thursday, July 1

The day of the opera George was tense, but exhilarated. He was good at planning and he had planned carefully for every part of the day and evening. The evening before he had spent time tucked into the shadows of the porch of the Victorian house across the way from Grace's condo. The house had long ago been turned into apartments and a flight of stairs to the doors brought them level with the open and undraped front window of Grace's condo. He'd waited until dark and parked two blocks away. After ascending the steps, he'd loosened the bulb in the light fixture and huddled back into the corner. He knew there was a chance that someone would go in or out while he was there, but he had a story ready if that should happen. He'd ask for an address in the next block and pretend to be lost. He was lucky, though. Nobody exited or entered the darkened building in the half-hour he spent watching Grace through the window. It was kind of mesmerizing to gaze into someone's life when they thought they were alone. He'd always found it fascinating that people in San Francisco who lived on upper floors often left their shades open and driving or walking by at night was like gazing into a fishbowl. The art on the walls, the books in the bookcases, sometimes people staring out their windows at the passersby as though they were invisible themselves.

In this case, there wasn't a lot to see. He had chosen the same time he was expected to be at the opera so that he could get an idea of the traffic and activity of her neighbors. She was watching TV and got up once and went toward the back of the space, turning a light on and leaving it on as she entered another room. He figured she went to pee and didn't bother to close the bathroom door. When she returned, she opened the fridge, grabbed a can of something, and returned to the couch. She got a phone call but didn't stay on long and spent some time playing on her phone. Nobody left or entered any of the neighboring condos, and only a couple of people walked past on the street below. It was so quiet that he got bored quickly and, unable to resist, used his phone to take a couple of surreptitious photos of her. It gave him a frisson of excitement to know that he would have those pictures, after all was done. He walked down the steps without being seen and drove home, going over his plans again and again, to assure he had left nothing to chance.

This week's Datebook section of the *Chronicle* had extensively reviewed the production of *Il Trovatore* they would be attending on Thursday. He knew the story well and noted some of the specifics of the sets and performances, in case anyone should ask.

On Thursday morning Amélie was excited at the prospect of impressing her friend with their great season-ticket seats. George capped off her enthusiasm by mentioning he'd made reservations for the three of them to meet two other couples at Absinthe for an early dinner. He wanted to make sure there were plenty of people who could say exactly where he had been all evening, not that he expected to ever need an alibi.

At the office he had closed his door and calculated everything stowed in his desk. One hundred thousand dollars plus an additional forty-five hundred in cash, several items he could sell or pawn, primarily gifts from Amélie's family or things he had picked up when visiting friends. It was amazing how many expensive things wealthy people left just lying around on tables and bookshelves. Anything that disappeared was automatically chalked up to the staff. Everyone knew you couldn't get decent help anymore. It wasn't enough to keep him going for long, but he figured if Amélie dumped him, he'd be able to keep working for a few months. It wouldn't look good if Dixon got rid of him right away. Much too political. Besides, he had connections with some of the firm's best clients, and he could expect the other forty thousand in cash from Gari soon. Just to be safe he called and left Gari a message reminding him that his sister would want the rest of the money. He was grateful that he and Amélie had never signed a pre-nuptial agreement. Technically, her mother's trust was hers, and they shared the house. Her inheritance from her father was still up in the air but would come to court soon and would be more significant if Grace was out of the way. He hadn't planned it this way, but maybe him taking Amélie to court to get custody of the kids would give him a bargaining chip on any settlement they made.

He didn't really believe that Amélie would file for divorce. Once all the estate nonsense was settled, he knew that she would be excited with his new venture. He took the well-worn real estate brochure out once more and thumbed through it, imagining Amélie and himself living the dream of owning the winery.

It had always surprised George that so many of the opera attendees dressed so informally. He liked to make a big deal of dressing the part, but he imagined they thought it was gauche to dress up for something so commonplace to them. Some of them showed up in jeans, with maybe a blazer, but not a tie. George always wore a suit and insisted that Amélie dress nicely, as well. If he was going to pay thousands of dollars a year for season seats, he was going to be remembered.

Amélie's school friend, Manon, was sitting stone-faced in the living room when George arrived home. He was certain Amélie had told her she was considering divorce and she was doing her best not to look at him with an expression that betrayed her disgust. He was pretty sure she'd commiserated with his wife, but only after pointing out her error in marrying beneath her station.

Feeling somewhat mischievous he deliberately greeted Manon warmly and insisted on giving her the customary hug and cheek kisses. It was fun to have her pull back from him and scowl at the affectations.

He was already feeling excited and it gave him an even bigger thrill to know that nobody had any idea of what he was up to. Losers, morons, who the hell named their kid Manon, for crying out loud?

One of his favorite pre-opera eateries was Absinthe, in Hayes Valley, and he had made special arrangements to assure a conspicuous table for his party. Stopping by during the lunch crush and greasing the skids with a generous gratuity had worked wonders.

George's final stop before heading out was in Amélie's craft room. He located the stack of family photos on the worktable, grabbed a few, and stuffed them in an envelope. He'd emailed Grace that he would be stopping by to drop off some family photos and she had let him know she would be at home.

Amélie and Manon were whispering over glasses of sherry when he came back down the stairs. He shrugged off the sudden stop in the conversation. Who the hell cared, anyway?

At the restaurant he dropped the ladies off to park the car. He waited a few minutes because he wanted to make an entrance that would ensure that everyone noticed he was there.

Dinner was the standard, upscale California cuisine, and he was gregarious and charming. He took the opportunity to show off his wine knowledge and ordered impressive bottles of red and white for the table. He waved at everyone he knew as they passed by and went table-to-table during dessert saying hello to people he hadn't spoken to in years.

The capper was that he picked up the check for the whole table. If Amélie hadn't had more than her usual limit of wine, she'd have probably fainted from the shock. But she laughed it off, and the covert glances she gave him echoed those he'd seen from her in the early days of their relationship. For a moment he wondered if a little more effort might save his marriage.

At the opera house George accompanied his friends to their seats and stayed until the lights flashed to let them know the performance was about to start. Before making his way to his seat he leaned down and whispered in Amélie's ear, "Be sure to order me a glass of champagne at the break and I'll meet you all at the bar."

CHAPTER TWENTY

Thursday, July 1

George had been careful when he chose his single seat. It was on another level, far in the back, near an exit. He made his way there and settled in just as the lights went down and the music started. Halfway into the overture, he began coughing intermittently, then more often and more violently. He continued until the people seated around him began to turn in their seats and give him "the glare." Right on cue he rose to compose himself in the lobby.

When he reached the lobby, he showed the usher his ticket and said he realized he'd left his inhaler in the car and confirmed he'd be able to return to the program after he'd retrieved it. Then he slipped out the side door and made a sharp right on Fulton Street.

It was just a few blocks to Grace's condo, but he hadn't taken into account the darkness and the unfamiliar street along the subsidized housing blocks. As he walked, he began to feel uncomfortable about the darkened streets and the number of homeless people that approached him. A knot of young Black men on the sidewalk untangled itself to let him pass and, though he didn't look back, he could feel them watching his progress up the hill.

It gave George a bit of a thrill to make this a cloak-and-dagger affair. He hoped that meeting Grace like this, showing her a few family photos, and shutting down her curiosity, would resolve everything, but he had the offer of money on his side, and he'd convinced himself that he was willing to make some sort of threat, if necessary, although he had no real idea what that threat might be.

Finally, he reached the condo complex and stood in the shadows until he was sure that there were no cars or passersby on the street, then he proceeded up the steps.

Before he knocked on the door, he pulled on his driving gloves. The door was slightly ajar and creaked open a bit when he knocked. Grace did not answer so he pushed on it gently and stuck his head into the room. "Grace?"

A bottle of wine and two glasses sat on the coffee table.

He slid into the room and closed the door quietly behind him. "Grace?"

From that point everything seemed to move both quickly and slowly. He had always been good at thinking on his feet and he was able to do what needed to do in just a few minutes.

When he returned to the door, he looked back over the living room. He hadn't realized he was panting until then, but he reached out his gloved hand to the wall to steady himself and took several deep breaths. He turned back to the coffee table and scooped up the open laptop and cell phone that lay there before he returned to the door.

Once he had settled down, he glanced around the room to assure he'd left no traces of his visit, his gaze resting on Grace's body lying on the floor beyond the coffee table, then he turned out the turned off the overhead light.

He switched off the porch light that Grace had left on and eased out onto the stair landing. There were no pedestrians on the sidewalk and he waited while a couple of cars passed on the street.

When all was quiet, he slipped down the dark stairs, and sticking close under the shadow of the hedge, made his way down to the street.

His time was running short, but he didn't want to walk past the darkened houses on Fulton Street again, so he walked quickly up to Hayes Street and turned left. His heart pounded, but he thought not so much in fear as in exhilaration. He just needed to dump the electronics on his way back to the opera house, but not look too hurried as he made his way down Hayes. The eateries were packed and the traffic on this street felt more like camouflage than risk. He spotted a trash can on the street, but then saw that a homeless man had stationed himself next to it.

"Hey, buddy." Squatting down he waved his hand in front of the man's face but didn't get much of a response. The guy was pretty out of it. "Hey, here's twenty bucks if you'll let me stick this stuff in your bag."

The man stirred to look at the laptop in George's hand. "Whaddya wanna do that for?" he slurred.

"Listen, just take it back wherever you go at night and dump it, or sell it, or whatever you want."

The man didn't seem to understand what George was saying, but George was beginning to feel like he was drawing attention to himself. He stuffed the wadded bill into the man's limp hand. "Here, fella, let me help you with your stuff." George spoke more loudly. He slid the laptop and phone into the man's backpack and pulled him awkwardly to his feet. He handed the pack to the man, who continued to stare down uncomprehendingly at the money in his hand. "Where're we going?" he mumbled.

"Well, I'm going to my home, and you are going to your home." The man nodded, turned away, and started down the sidewalk, toward some unknown destination.

George continued along the street, making the best time that he could.

He entered the lobby of the opera house as the applause signaling the end of the second act erupted. He took off his coat and stuffed the gloves into the pocket, returning them to his empty seat and progressing quickly to the bar.

Amélie and Manon had made their way to the lobby and Amélie stood holding two flutes of champagne.

"This stuff is really terrible for the price, but you said to order it," she said as she handed him the glass. "You look flushed, are you okay?"

"Fine, I'm fine, just hot where I was sitting."

He took a large swallow of the wine and winced at the acrid taste.

His heart rate had slowed by now and he was feeling pretty satisfied with himself.

CHAPTER TWENTY-ONE

Saturday, July 3

Detective Burns took a minute to look around him before ringing the bell. It was not much different since he'd last been here, although the half-dead petunias in the brick flowerbed looked to be replacements for the previous half-dead plants. The door still needed painting, the dust still clung to the windowpane in the door, backed by the limp IKEA curtain. Kestrel had never been much of a housekeeper. It was kind of nice to see that some things hadn't changed.

He rang the bell and waited for a response. Nothing. Looked like the doorbell still didn't work. Kestrel's landlady and mother, Victoria, was a big fan of deferred maintenance.

He knocked firmly. No sound came from the other side of the door, but the door to the adjoining unit popped open.

"Hey, Bobby." Sam didn't try to hide his surprise at seeing Bobby there after so long.

"Sam." The word hung between them; what else was there to say?

"Um, I think she's in there. Try knocking again." Sam nodded toward the door and then turned away letting his door close behind him.

Bobby knocked again, a little more forcefully this time and after a long pause the dingy curtain twitched back a bit and the door swung open.

It was apparent he had woken Kestrel up. Her sleepy smile and bed hair topped a huge Grateful Dead T-shirt that barely served to maintain decent door-opening requirements.

"Bobby, wow. Long time no see." She gave him an appraising look and stepped back, letting the door open wider. She lifted her cheek to him for the mandatory kiss of old friends. "What are you doing here?"

"It's a semi-official visit, K." Bobby stepped in, ignoring her upraised face.

"Really? What did I do wrong this time?" Her smile faltered a bit in confusion. "I don't think I've pissed off the powers-that-be lately. I've been careful not to mention the police chief in my blog."

"Good, but this is something different."

"Let me go put on something more presentable for official police business." She continued to smile but backed quickly out of the kitchen, aware that the oversized shirt covered even less in the back.

Previously Bobby would have popped a pod into the coffee machine and made himself at home at the tiny kitchen table, but for now he simply closed the door behind him and waited for her to return.

Kestrel wasn't gone long but returned with a pair of yoga pants completing her ensemble, and her hair combed and pulled into a scrunchy at the back. It looked like she'd dashed the sleep from her eyes with a bit of cold water, although her eyes still looked a little tired.

"Sorry to wake you up. Were you working last night?"

"Yeah, you know me, no rest for the wicked. So, what's up?"

"Just a new case I caught yesterday. Thought you might have some information."

"I thought you were in Homicide now." She still looked confused.

"I am. It's a recent homicide. Looks like you might know the victim."

"Someone I know?" There was an edge of panic in the question and he could see that her sleepy brain was springing awake as she ran through the names of people she knew who might have been killed.

He'd pulled out his notebook and flipped it open. "Yes, a woman named Grace Callahan. Lived over near Alamo Square."

Bobby looked up at the strangled sound that came from Kestrel. She had not moved but the shock on her face was evident. She reached out to steady herself on the back of the kitchen chair.

"Grace?"

"K, sit down a minute. Do you want some water or something?" Bobby pulled out the chair for her and she sank into it.

Kestrel did not speak but seemed stunned. She rocked gently back and forth, staring forward, her hands clasped in her lap.

Bobby pulled out the other chair and turned it to face her. He sat and took her hands in his.

"Who is Grace Callahan to you, K? I never heard you mention her."

"We just met… just one time." There was a sadness in Kestrel's voice that he'd never heard before.

"But who was she?"

"Grace was my sister." Kestrel's voice had faded to a whisper.

"You never mentioned a sister before."

"I just found her, we just found each other… and now she's gone."

Bobby felt awful. He'd had plenty of training and experience with breaking this kind of news to family, but he'd not been prepared today. He'd come here to find out why Kestrel's fingerprints were all over a dead woman's condo, not to tell someone they'd lost family.

Bobby thought back to when he'd stood over the crumpled body in the Fulton Street condo. There had been a twinge of recognition of the dead woman but he'd passed it off to being human enough to not be able to look at a person whose life had been stolen, without regret.

"I don't understand, K. How could she be your sister?"

"It was just some weird results from a DNA test. One minute you're alone with your crazy mother and the next thing you know there's someone who looks like you and laughs like you and, and, I don't know." Kestrel had buried her face in her hands and begun to quietly sob.

Bobby realized he was going to have to step back from this case. That he shouldn't be here. Someone else was going to have to ask these questions, figure out the connections.

He would need to be here for his friend and it wasn't ethical or right for him to be here alone with her, at this point their only suspect.

Bobby pulled his phone from his pocket and punched a contact number. It rang twice before he got an answer. "Lieutenant, I have a problem here." He grabbed a wad of paper towels and handed them to Kestrel. "I'm going to need some backup."

CHAPTER TWENTY-TWO

Saturday, July 3

Detective Raquel "Rocky" Stafford swerved her car into the left lane, making an illegal U-turn to avoid stalled traffic. She was in no mood to put up with tourists or Uber drivers. On her way to her latest call, she was having a bit of a problem keeping things in perspective. Bobby Burns, the hot detective she'd gone out on a limb to ask out for a drink last night, was in a "situation," whatever the hell that meant.

For months she and Burns had been flirting and skirting the issue of who would most like to get into whose pants. Yesterday she'd jumped into the twenty-first century and asked Detective Burns out for a drink. Once she'd confirmed that she would be transferring to Vice at the end of the month she'd decided to take a shot at getting to know him better. Generally, you didn't want to be bedding other officers in your department, but now that she would be moving elsewhere, it seemed like the perfect time to send up the flare signaling "I think you are hot and this is your chance." No conflicts, no concerns, let's just get into the hot and heavy; your place or mine?

Up to that point he'd been open, funny, cute, hot, and all the adjectives that would normally land him in her bed before long, but last night he'd withdrawn on her. He'd shown up all right, but he'd been aloof, distracted, and generally a total bust as far as hooking up had gone. Instead of ending up in either of their apartments, he'd been distant and unresponsive. Prince Charming had left his dimples at home. WTF? Now she might find out why, although it didn't help much.

It was her day off and she'd been prepping for a casual lunch with her new boss in Vice. Casual as in not at a fancy place, but dressy in that she was wearing a nice dress, blazer, and shoes with actual heels and straps that showed off her shapely ankles. The call came from her current boss, Captain Balboa, and the lunch was summarily cancelled. She'd been instructed to get to a suspect's location ASAP, but not before she'd looked up the records for Kestrel Jonas, the wannabe investigative reporter who'd broken the big police commissioner cover-up last year. The records were skimpy but it seemed like Ms. Jonas had happened on some shady dealings and bad guys in her usual occupation of digging up dirt on the San Francisco elite. Her arrest and the trumped-up charges brought against her after the story broke had poured gasoline on a City Hall already putting out wildfires as fast as they could. Eventually, she'd been cleared, if not loved, by the police, and now her fingerprints had shown up all over a murder scene. Captain Balboa had taken five minutes to bring her up to date on Bobby Burns' role in all this and the bad spot he'd accidentally gotten himself into.

Burns had been sent to the crime scene to investigate, got the fingerprint report from the CSI team, and taken it upon himself to go see Jonas. Once he was there, he realized his previous relationship with Jonas, that had started after she had been arrested, put him out of the running for leading this investigation. Rocky had checked out Jonas's mug shot. White chick, late twenties, kind of hot, but nothing special.

Now an SOS for backup in a sticky situation had gone out from Bobby Burns. Balboa had been vague on the whole thing, mostly because he had no idea how sticky it might be. Burns picks up a homicide, fingerprints in the files, ex-girlfriend is sister of victim. Speed out there and see what you can find out.

That made it a little complicated for Rocky, as well. It wasn't like she was begging for dates, but she really liked Bobby. They'd been working together ever since Rocky had moved back to the San Francisco Bay Area from Los Angeles and the two had hit it off from the start. Rocky had plenty of offers if she was looking for them. She was successful, beautiful, if a little on the assertive side, a police detective with a lot of homicide experience and on the verge of moving into Vice with an enviable promotion, somewhat of a breakthrough for a Black woman on the SFPD. Getting to this point had taken a whole lot of work and struggle, from her childhood in Oakland, her top-of-class ranking from the Police Academy, and fighting her way with grit and humor through years of prejudice and grunt work on the forces in San Diego and Los Angeles. She really didn't need this shit!

Two more blocks to the address and she still didn't know how she felt about the whole thing.

She slid her car into a parking spot and took a minute to figure out what the hell was going on. She saw Burns' car on the other side of the street. What she knew was that Bobby had been called to a homicide yesterday on Fulton Street near Alamo Square. No big surprises there until the fingerprints in the apartment turned up his ex-girlfriend.

Now he was sitting in the cozy kitchen of his ex, wondering how he'd become involved in her sister's murder, and how could he not have known it was her sister if they'd had such a hot and heavy relationship? Rocky had been sent to assure there was no question of bias in the investigation.

Rocky had also taken the time to look over the notes and forensics reports. No break-in, victim had let the killer into her apartment. There was no sign of a struggle, no murder weapon, no witnesses, so far; just a dead lady and a missing phone and computer.

When Rocky knocked on the door, she noted the curtain at the adjoining unit flicking back for a second. Curious neighbors could sometimes be very useful.

The door opened, and Rocky quickly assessed the woman before her. Young-looking, no makeup, tall, slim, and pale. The pale might have come from having the police there, but Rocky thought the girl didn't probably attract a lot of attention, especially dressed as she was. It was obvious she'd been crying and she held a wad of soggy paper towels in her hand.

Rocky's glance swept the room and found Bobby standing on the far side, next to the counter. He looked like he'd backed as far out of the room as possible without running away. No surprise there, nobody wants to be suspected of covering anything up.

"Ms. Jonas? I'm Detective Stafford of the SFPD." Rocky pulled her blazer aside to show the badge on a lanyard around her neck. "May I come in?"

Kestrel mumbled something and stepped back so Rocky could enter.

CHAPTER TWENTY-THREE

Saturday, July 3

Rocky took in the room, nothing special, but better than her own apartment. Real estate in San Francisco was a joke for the working class. She was making more money than she'd ever dreamed of and could barely afford a studio-plus walk-up. She wondered how a freelance writer could afford what looked to be a two-bedroom with some view and private parking.

"I'm going to have Detective Burns bring me up to date and then I'll have a few questions for you."

"Okay." Kestrel shot Bobby a pleading glance that bounced off him as he focused on Rocky.

"Why don't we all sit down?" Rocky pulled a chair out from the kitchen table and made herself comfortable. She focused her attention on Burns but made sure she could see Kestrel's reactions.

"Detective Burns, I understand you were called to a suspected murder scene yesterday about, let's see, two p.m. Is that correct?" Rocky referred to the notes she'd made at headquarters.

"Yes, that's right. I was next up on the rotation and I headed out right away." Bobby seemed to relax a bit, realizing that Rocky knew what she was doing and would be thorough.

"Who else was at the scene when you arrived at 988 Fulton Street?"

"Officer Regan was waiting at the door of the condo. There was a traffic guy and the Forensics van showed up right after me."

The questions continued up to the point where Bobby had arrived at Kestrel's apartment and asked her if she knew Grace Callahan.

"Did you and Ms. Jonas have any other discussion after she identified Grace Callahan as her sister?"

"No, ma'am." The formality of the response surprised Rocky, but she chalked it up to this being the first time Bobby had been interviewed by a Homicide cop.

Rocky took a few moments to run back over her notes and then she turned to Kestrel.

The girl had followed the discussion carefully, looking at each of them when they spoke, but had not reacted to the questions until the last one when Rocky mentioned Grace. She did not start crying again, but she looked a little dazed.

"Do you want to get a drink of water or something before we start?"

"Um, yeah. I'd like some coffee. Can I make some for all of us?"

Rocky nodded and watched the girl move around the kitchen making the coffee. When three full cups had been placed on the table and they'd assured her they didn't need cream or sugar, Rocky started her questions. She took out her recorder and turned it on.

"I am going to record this interview so that I don't have to be taking notes. Are you okay with that?"

Kestrel nodded.

"Can you give a verbal affirmation, Ms. Jonas? I need it on the recorder."

"Yes, it is okay to record me."

"Thank you. Can you tell me what you do for a living?"

"I actually have a lot of jobs. I am a free-lance reporter, and I have a blog about San Francisco. I work at a couple of different places in the city as serving staff."

"What places do you work?"

"At the Pacific Union Club and at The Towers, and sometimes at the Bohemian Club for special events. It doesn't pay very much, but it is good research for the blog."

Rocky looked around the kitchen. "It is pretty expensive to live in San Francisco. How do you afford it with those type of jobs?"

"I work a lot of shifts." Kestrel had gotten a defensive tone in her voice. "I don't pay much rent because my mom owns this building. It's not free, but it is not as much as the other tenant pays."

"So, Ms. Jonas, you said that the victim, Grace Callahan, was your sister, but that you just met. Can you clarify that for me?"

For a moment Rocky thought Kestrel might start crying, but the woman just took a deep breath. "Well, until just the other day I didn't know I had a sister, or any family other than my mom and grandmother. Then I did this Heritage thing and I found out that I did have a sister and a half-brother."

"This Heritage thing?"

"You know, where you order a kit from Heritage and then you send them a vial of spit and they analyze it and link you up to people you are related to. Like they advertise on television."

"Yes, I've seen those ads. So, you sent them your spit, uh, saliva sample?"

"Yes, I bought the kit a while ago when I was kind of drunk and mad at my mom, but then I decided to send it in. They take weeks and weeks to get the results back to you and I'd almost forgotten about it."

"Why?" Bobby said. He'd been following the discussion with interest. A withering look from Rocky set him back in his chair and he clamped his lips shut.

"Just because I wasn't pissed anymore and I figured there wouldn't be anything there. Then when I opened it, I couldn't believe it said I had a sister. I mean, I guess I always thought maybe my dad had married again and had kids with someone else, but this wasn't a half-sister. This was a sister from the same mom and dad."

"What did you do when you read that?"

"I sent an email to her, to Grace, and we arranged to meet. After we met, I went to my mom and asked her what the hell was going on. She said she had given her first child up for adoption, and then she had me with the same man. But he was not who I thought my dad was."

"What did your dad say about all this?"

"I don't even know who my dad is. My mom made up some name and told me that was my dad. Paul Jonas, he doesn't even exist." Kestrel had started to tear up and her voice had become shrill with indignation.

"Did the Heritage results you got tell you who your dad really is?"

"No, because he isn't in the database. There is a half-brother there, but I don't know who he is. It's not like they publish a directory with names and addresses. Besides, I just wasn't that interested in him, I was really only interested in my sister." The tears had started and the final words were choked out.

Bobby had scooted his chair closer to Kestrel and put his arm around her shoulders, ignoring the glare from Rocky.

"Okay, let's take a break for a minute. Can I talk to you outside, Detective Burns?"

Rocky strode out the door and turned suddenly on Bobby as he came out behind her.

"What is wrong with you, Bobby? You can't go around hugging a suspect in a murder investigation. Do you want to get caught up in some scandal?"

Bobby bridled at her words, but then had the good grace to look abashed. "I'm sorry, you just don't know about Kestrel and her mom. This is hard for her."

"Yeah, I know you have all the inside information, but let me get the story myself. If you can't step back, you're going to have to leave the interview, get it?"

"Yeah, I get it."

"Okay, then. Let's see if we can get the rest of the story."

When they re-entered the kitchen, Kestrel had gotten herself another cup of coffee, although she had hesitated over the open bottle of wine on the counter for a moment first. Her eyes were red but the tears had stopped.

CHAPTER TWENTY-FOUR

Saturday, July 3

Before starting again Rocky took a sip of the sludgy black coffee and winced a bit. It was almost as bad as the stuff at the station.

"What did you do to get connected with your sister, with Ms. Callahan?"

"Well, you don't have real contact information from Heritage, but you can send a message to the people who show up in your family, so I sent her a message and said I thought we might be sisters. After a couple of days, she sent me a message back telling me that she lived in San Francisco and asking where I was."

"And then what?"

"Well, I told her a little about me. My name and where I lived. I told her I had grown up with my mom, *our* mom, and didn't know my dad or that I had a sister. She wrote back and said she'd been adopted and grew up on the Peninsula."

"How did the two of you meet?"

"I don't think either of us had any idea how to take all of this. She suggested we might meet someplace and see how it went, so we decided to meet at the Academy of Sciences and see what happened."

"When was this meeting?"

"Last Tuesday."

"*Tuesday*, two days before she was murdered?"

"I guess, but I didn't know when she was killed."

"You met at the Academy of Sciences in Golden Gate Park, right?"

"Yes, we decided to meet at about noon. I had to work until eleven Wednesday. At the club, the Pacific Union Club."

"What did you do after you got off work?"

"I took the bus to the park and walked to the Academy."

"How were you supposed to recognize Ms. Callahan? Did you pick a specific place to meet?"

"She told me we should meet in the entry hall, you know, where you pay to get in."

"Did you see her right away?"

"Um, actually I got there a little early so I could watch her come in."

"Why did you do that?"

Kestrel hesitated for a moment. "Well, I just wanted to see what she was like. What she was wearing. I brought some different clothes with me in a bag."

"You brought a change of clothes?"

"I was getting off work and wearing my sort of uniform, Black pants and a white shirt and comfortable shoes. If she was dressed up, I didn't want to look like some poor relation or something. I was nervous."

"You were nervous about meeting your sister?"

"Yes, excited, but nervous about what she would think of me."

"What was Ms. Callahan wearing when you saw her enter the Academy?"

"She looked nice, kind of shy, and she was wearing a black skirt and a nice blouse. She had on shoes with little heels, but I could tell they were expensive ones, not like from Ross or someplace."

"How did you know it was her?" For the first time there was some interest in Rocky's voice. She really did wonder how this would work, meeting someone like that for the first time.

"Because she looked just like me, only better." For a moment it seemed like Kestrel would start crying again, but she took a deep shuddering breath and continued. "She looked like I might look if I ate healthy food, worked out, paid more than twenty bucks for a haircut, and bought my skin stuff at Nordstrom's instead of CVS. She was who I wanted to be."

"Did that bother you, that you thought she was better than you?"

"No, I was glad. It meant that I didn't have to just be me, I could be like her."

Rocky jumped when Bobby spoke, she'd almost forgotten that he was there.

"I thought it was you when I went to the scene. I thought it was you dead on the floor." He didn't try to disguise the anguish in his voice.

The look Rocky shot him was not so much angry as acknowledging. She couldn't imagine going to a scene where she thought someone she knew was the victim. But still, it hurt just a bit to know he still cared.

Rocky moved on quickly. "What did you do when you saw her?"

"I was behind a pillar on the right side of the entry when she came in and I went into the bathroom and quickly changed my clothes. I had brought a couple of outfits, but one was kind of like hers; a skirt and blouse, flats, simple jewelry."

"What did you do after you changed your clothes?"

"I kind of snuck past her and checked my bag at the coat check thing. I didn't want to be carrying a bag around with me."

"Do you have the coat check tag?"

"Maybe, my purse and pockets are full of all kinds of crap until I purge it all."

"What happened after you checked your bag?"

"Actually, I thought about leaving. It was really hard to walk up to her. I could see she was checking her watch and I think she'd almost decided to go ahead into the exhibits but decided to wait for a bit more. I walked up behind her and just said her name. I just said… 'Grace.' She turned quickly, like she was nervous, too. Then she just threw her arms around me. She told me she knew I would come."

At this point, the tears started up again, and Rocky thought it might be a good time to take a break. "Okay, I'm going to stop for a minute and check in at the precinct."

Rocky stepped out onto the porch and noticed the twitch of the curtain next door. She'd made it sound official, but her first call was to her older sister. The call didn't last long and if Buzzy was surprised to hear from her, she didn't let on.

Rocky didn't know what to think, about Kestrel and Grace, about Bobby Burns, about her own family. For just a moment she wished her transfer had been completed and this case hadn't come to her. Police work wasn't like "Law and Order" on television. It was gather the facts, make the connections. It had nothing to do with shitty childhoods, or old romances, or discovering you weren't who you thought you were. She'd never have believed how relieved she felt *to know* who she was and where she came from. She did call into headquarters to assure she'd not been assigned to some easier case in the interim, but, no... she was still figuring out WTF for Kestrel Jonas, Grace Callahan, and Bobby Burns.

CHAPTER TWENTY-FIVE

Saturday, July 3

Kestrel had calmed down by the time Rocky returned to the kitchen. Bobby was still out on the deck smoking a cigarette. She'd thought he had quit but knew that quitting was a relative term. She wished she had a cigarette herself right now.

"Is it okay to start again, Ms. Jonas?" Rocky surreptitiously looked at her watch. This interview was taking up a lot of the afternoon, not that she had any place better to be.

"Can you call me Kestrel, or Kay? Ms. Jonas sounds so weird, especially since Paul Jonas is a fantasy."

"I can call you Kestrel." Rocky was surprised at the sweet smile Kestrel gave her. It almost made her feel suspicious. Maybe she'd been a cop too long.

"Do we need to wait for Bobby?" Kestrel nodded toward the deck where Detective Burns still prowled, spewing cigarette smoke with each pacing pass.

"No, Detective Burns is secondary on this case, unless there is something you want to clarify about your relationship with him."

"You mean other than it is ancient history?"

"No, I mean… I don't know what I mean. Never mind."

"I know what you mean. Bobby and I are done. It was a mistake to begin with. I can't take his stiff neck and he wasn't ready for my drama."

"I don't need to know this."

"I think maybe you do. Bobby is my friend. He supported me when my life sucked, but we crossed a line we should never have crossed. If we are lucky, we will be able to stay friends but, he needs someone who understands who he is and what he does, and I need someone a little… looser."

Bobby slid the door open and stepped into the room.

"I'm just turning the recorder back on, Detective Burns. Ms. Jonas, Kestrel, what happened after Ms. Callahan hugged you?"

"I was kind of shocked, but I held her really tight for a minute. I never had family other than my mom and grandma. It felt good."

"Then what?"

"She had already paid for us both to go in, so we started looking at the exhibits. We didn't say much at first. What was there to say, really? I hadn't been there since they remodeled and really wanted to go to the aquarium and see how it was different. After a while she started talking about what it was like to be adopted and what her parents were like. They lived near Palo Alto where my grandma lived, and she went to a private school there and then to Stanford. I'd spent a lot of summers there with Gran and even went to Paly, Palo Alto High School, for a while and we knew a lot of the same places."

"Did she do all the talking?"

"No, I told her how lucky she was that my mom gave her up for adoption. My life was nothing like hers. She was really wanted, and I always wondered why my mom kept me. It seemed like she didn't want me at all but was stuck with me."

"Did that make you angry?"

"Maybe, a little. Mostly it made me sad."

Kestrel seemed to be deflating at this point and Rocky decided to cut to the chase.

"Did you go to Grace Callahan's home on Tuesday?"

"Yes, after we wandered around a bit, we had some lunch, and some wine. Then she asked me if I wanted to see her place. I guess she had wanted to make sure I wasn't too weird before she invited me to her condo. I said yes, and we took an Uber over to Fulton Street."

"What did you do when you got to her condo?"

"I was supposed to go to work at The Towers that night, but I called in sick, so we sat around and drank more wine. We had some food she had in the fridge: cheese and crackers, whatever was there. I ended up spending the night crashed on her sofa."

"What time did you leave on Wednesday?"

"We woke up early and I took the bus back here to get ready for work. I worked early at the PU Club and then did a dinner shift at The Towers."

"Do you have witnesses that you were at the, what is it, The Towers all evening?"

"Yeah, I didn't think of them as witnesses, but tons of people saw me there that night. I got home about ten o'clock. Sam, next door, probably heard me come in, but I didn't see him."

"Do you know who Grace was expecting Thursday night?"

"Yes, she said she was going to meet with the guy she met before, our half-brother."

"Your half-brother? Is this someone else from the Heritage thing?"

"Yes, Grace got her results before I got mine, so I didn't show up on her Heritage when she first got it. Just our half-brother. Grace said she had sent an email and they met for dinner. She didn't like him; he kind of creeped her out. But he was supposed to bring some family pictures for her to see on Thursday night." Kestrel seemed to suddenly realize she might know something that would help. "I would have his information in my Heritage account, too. I wasn't interested in contacting him, so I never did, but she described him to me."

"Do you have the emails you exchanged with Ms. Callahan?"

"Yes, I have them, there were only a couple, but they are in my account."

Rocky wanted to check on some things before she continued the interview. She stood up. "I'd like to take your computer and have it checked over."

Kestrel paled and shot a furtive look at Detective Burns. "I can't let you have my computer. I can print the emails and reports or give you the Heritage account password, but there's private stuff in my computer."

"What could be that private? We're the police, we'll return everything to you in a couple of days."

"No, you really can't take my computer. My contacts and sources are in there and all my research for my articles and my blog." Kestrel stood up and strode to the kitchen door. She swung it open and banged loudly on the neighbor's door. "Sam, Sam, are you in there? I need you right away." She kept knocking and even kicked the door a couple of times before it opened.

"What the hell is going on?" Sam looked rumpled, like he'd been sleeping and looked from Kestrel to Rocky, and then past Rocky to Bobby.

"These are the police. They want to take my computer and I can't let them have it. You're a lawyer. Do I have to let them take it?"

Sam ran his hands through his hair and then placed one big paw on Kestrel's shoulder. "Just relax a minute, let me find out what is going on and we can all decide what we need to do."

It was surprising how quickly Kestrel had calmed down in response to Sam's quiet tone. He looked at Rocky. "Let me get my shoes on and I'll be right over."

CHAPTER TWENTY-SIX

Saturday, July 3

Bobby could barely keep up with Rocky's stride going back to her car. How does she walk that fast in heels?

When she reached her car, she swung the door open and turned to him. "Get in," she barked.

"My car is right across the street."

"Get the fuck into the fucking car," she spoke through gritted teeth.

Considering that discretion was the better part of valor, Bobby did as he was told.

Once he was in his seat with the door closed, she turned her full fury on him.

"What just happened in there?"

"It wasn't your fault, you were blindsided."

"Tell me about it. What is going on?"

"I didn't know they would send you out here on this case, but I should have guessed. You're the only detective in Homicide who can handle this."

"What are you talking about, Bobby? This is not funny." Rocky's voice had continued to rise.

"Just relax a minute and I will tell you what I know."

"Okay." Rocky took a deep breath and adjusted her shoulders. "Just tell me."

"Before you came on the force last year there was a big shake-up in the department. It brought down the commissioner and went all the way to the mayor's office."

"Yeah, I know, I heard. So what? What does that have to do with this case?"

"Nothing to do with the case, but a lot to do with Kestrel Jonas and her laptop."

"I don't get it."

"Kestrel is a freelance journalist."

Rocky snorted and rolled her eyes.

"I know, she's kind of flaky, and works as a food server, and has a tacky blog that exposes the upper class to a lot of angst, but she also has a lot of contacts, *a lot* of contacts."

"You're saying this has something to do with the 'big purge'?"

"She had everything to do with it. She stumbled across the dirt, dug it up, shaped it into a killer story, and broke it right over the head of the commissioner."

"That was a long time ago; why is it important now?"

"It isn't about this murder; it is about her computer. One of the big deals was that her information and her contacts were all in her computer. The big brass wanted to get their hands on the information and tried every trick in the book to force the issue. The courts, with the help of her attorney neighbor, Sam, decided that she and her computer were protected by the First Amendment."

"Okay, but why did they send *me* out here? I'll be gone from Homicide in a few weeks and I don't know anything about all of this."

"Yeah, well you are the only police officer in San Francisco who does not have a strong opinion about the purge and about Kestrel, one way or another."

"But, what about my transfer?"

"Guess you'd better solve this in the next few weeks."

"Fuck!" Bobby jumped when Rocky's fist hit the dashboard of the car. "I don't have time for this!"

Bobby and Rocky sat staring forward for several seconds.

"Why wasn't all this in the police reports?"

"It's there, but not where you can find it in a fifteen-minute review. You should have gone straight to Google. The whole thing would have spilled onto you."

Again, there was silence. "Is this how you got involved with her?" she asked.

"Yeah, I was in Internal Affairs then."

"You were in I.A.?"

"Yeah, well, I transferred to Homicide when I realized I would do better with dead bodies than dead careers."

The sun was going down and Karl the Fog had descended while they sat in silence.

Finally, Rocky spoke. "Get the hell out of my car. I'm going home."

As Rocky drove away Bobby looked back at the duplex. The light had gone on in Kestrel's kitchen. He considered going back but thought better of it. He didn't need the drama and suspected that Sam was probably sitting on the deck with her, sharing the always- available bottle of wine. He climbed into his car and headed through the clogged city streets toward home.

Bobby tried to shake off the hint of jealousy toward Kestrel and Sam's relationship. Sam wasn't any better for her than Bobby had been, but something about that woman just sucked you in. Bobby and Sam would always be like brothers to Kestrel: protective, anxious, frustrated, and annoyed. Why couldn't he just get into a nice simple relationship with a hot coroner, for crying out loud. There were even a couple of good-looking prison guards he'd dated, but no, he had to go for the lost-waif psycho type. It was his destiny.

He stopped at the corner bodega near his apartment and picked up a six-pack, and after a few conflicted moments, bought a fresh pack of cigarettes, then changed it to a carton. He figured he owed various cops and CSI guys at least a couple of packs since he had quit smoking. Now was not the time to become a better person. He just hoped he didn't end up being a worse one.

Bobby had been close to guessing the state of Kestrel and Sam, but the night had gotten chilly and they still sat at the kitchen table sharing the wine while Kestrel told him about the sister she'd almost had.

CHAPTER TWENTY-SEVEN

Saturday, July 3

As Rocky drove home through the slow traffic her cell phone rang and diverted to the car's Bluetooth. "Hey there, Mom. How are you doing?"

"I'm doing just fine, but I wondered when you would be here for dinner. I made all your favorites."

The comforting sound of her mother's voice calmed Rocky down a bit before she realized she was headed for her silent apartment when she'd promised to have dinner with her family tonight.

She looked at her watch as she made another illegal U-turn to the sound of blaring horns. It was a hard habit to break.

"I'm in the car now, Mom. I should be there in about twenty minutes. You know, traffic this time of day."

"Oh, that's just fine. Buzzy and Albert just got here with the kids. So, we'll see you soon, right?"

"Yep, I'll be there in a flash."

Buzzy, Albert, and the kids, plus her freeloader brother and his annoying girlfriend. Sometimes Rocky wished she didn't know who her siblings were. She wondered what she would do if she suddenly found out she wasn't who she thought she was. She wasn't sure if it would be a dream come true, or a nightmare.

When she reached her mom's building in Oakland it had been quite a bit longer than the twenty minutes she had promised. She tried to park under a light to protect her car, but the old Toyota wasn't in much danger of being bothered. The CD player had been stolen the last time she was here, and the car looked right at home among the beaters parked around it. She made enough money now to get a better car, but it didn't seem worth the effort. She'd have to worry about it when she came to the old neighborhood and she suspected the new wheels would not be appreciated by her family. Mama would have been happy, but the rest of them, not so much. They had come to grips with her being a cop, but there was no need to flaunt her higher paycheck.

The elevator in the building was on the fritz, as usual, so she slogged herself up the three flights of stairs, greeted at each level by a different, unwelcome aroma. Old urine on the second floor, soggy cooked cabbage on the third, and then, on the fourth floor, marijuana smoke and collard greens. The legalization of pot in California had made visits home much less stressful, although she was pretty sure the joints shared by her siblings in the stairwell were still not of the legally sanctioned and taxed variety.

She hesitated outside the door for the few seconds it took to confirm that all the usual suspects had arrived. Two toddlers tried to out-scream each other and the ball game was turned up to drown them out. Her sister, Buzzy, was hollering at one of the kids, or her younger brother, or maybe at her husband. It didn't make much difference who was targeted, the shrill voice cut across all competition.

It always took Rocky a few minutes to acclimate to her family milieu. Since moving back to San Francisco, she spent most of her non-work life in her quiet apartment by herself. She had plenty of offers to go out, but she was drawn to the solitude of her own space. She owned a television, but she seldom turned it on. It mostly existed for streaming movies she'd meant to see at the theater but never made it. She had hundreds of music CDs and the stacks of books on her tables and chairs and beside the bed were quickly becoming a safety hazard.

She could imagine someone finding her crushed body under a stack of unread books while Billie Holliday and Edith Piaf looped interminably on her sound system.

She opened the door with the key that hung around her neck. Nobody in this neighborhood ever left their door unlocked, whether they were home or not. She and the other kids had started wearing the keys when they started school. She figured the term latchkey kid applied to almost everyone she'd ever known. If you were lucky, you were the first kid back from school and got the best pick of snacks and control of the TV remote until someone bigger came home.

She'd thought about knocking but knew she would never be heard. The doorbell in the center of the door, right below the ubiquitous peephole, dangled precariously by a wire. She took a moment to click it back into the empty slot. She couldn't recall if the doorbell had ever worked, but she didn't remember ever hearing it ring.

She figured she'd stick around long enough to have some of Mom's cooking, which mostly consisted of opening cans and boxes and combining them in filling and familiar ways, and then she'd beg early meetings and go home to that nice bottle of wine she'd been longing for.

It turned out that this was a family celebration, of sorts. Seems that Buzzy's son had finally been mostly potty-trained, and just in time for Buzzy to announce that she had another bun in the oven. Rocky couldn't figure out how the laid-back, not-too-bright Albert was able to support them all, but he came home every night and kept food on the table and a decent roof over their heads. It was more than her own father had managed. After two servings of macaroni and cheese (the kind in the blue box), greens, fried chicken from the freezer, and a huge chunk of German chocolate cake, she managed to escape from Oakland across the Bay Bridge to the foggy city. The one advantage to her sister's penchant for popping out babies on a regular basis was that her mother had pretty much given up on nagging her about when she was going to start having babies. Observing her brother Antonio's girlfriend during the evening she suspected that there would be another announcement of impending birth before long. Skinny Mirabelle was beginning to show but was probably holding out for a marriage proposal before announcing. Rocky was pretty sure that was wishful thinking on Mirabelle's part. Growing up, the joke had been that the most common neighborhood marriage proposal was "You're what!?"

On the bridge Karl's shifting billows closed behind her beat-up car and she allowed herself to relax.

CHAPTER TWENTY-EIGHT

Saturday, July 3

Kestrel closed the door behind Sam as he returned to his apartment. They'd finished the wine and she'd been tempted to open another bottle before Sam remembered he had someplace important to be the next day. She waited until his door closed before turning off the porch light. Leaving the unwashed glasses in the sink and the empty bottle on the table she turned out the kitchen light and fell onto the silky comforter on top of her bed.

***

Sam flipped on the dining room light and slumped into the only chair not stacked with files and books. The open file before him on the table displayed the angry face of a man with a lot to be angry about. Another quick and easy conviction of a Black man had landed the guy in prison for a crime Sam was trying to prove he didn't commit. Tomorrow he'd be driving across the Golden Gate and going to San Quentin to visit him with more papers and questions and appeals. This wasn't Sam's job, but it was his purpose. He shuffled through the papers for a few minutes and then pushed the file folder away.

There was no point in trying to get any additional work done. The bottle of wine and story of Kestrel's lost sister had drained him of his enthusiasm for social justice. He knew Kestrel's mother, Victoria, and he knew more than he wanted to about their painful relationship. This sister who had flitted into her life and out again so swiftly, making only a ripple on the surface, was a conundrum. People just didn't find a new reality and then drop back into the familiar discomfort of the old life. But, for tonight, his friend was drunk enough to sleep and had a busy day ahead of her that would prevent the kind of rumination he expected would eventually upend her life.

When he'd first moved into the duplex, he had spent much of his free time trying to catch a glimpse of Kestrel as she dashed in and out of her half of the building. She left early and came home late; she slept late on some days and stayed up all night sometimes. She seldom drove, but when she did it was an old rattletrap of a VW Bug. He finally got to meet her, using the ploy of giving her mis-delivered mail, after lying in wait for several hours for her to return home. The fact that he had waylaid the mail carrier to obtain the mail was a secret still known only to him.

She'd been excited to finally meet him and made it seem like he had been avoiding her all that time. She wasn't unfriendly, just very busy, and somewhat scattered. Her life was a juggling act of jobs, social media, and contacts. In between she drank too much and slept when she could. And she was completely mesmerizing to him. When she went to work she was different. One time he had run into her in the city going between her two jobs and didn't even recognize her until she spoke to him. That mousy woman in undistinguished clothing and clunky glasses was a world away from his intelligent, spunky neighbor.

There had been a bit of an early dalliance that he'd initially hoped would develop into something more. But, after a lot of sleepless nights, he'd realized that being sucked into her vortex kept him from focusing on his own career and projects. He wasn't the world's best attorney but he was dogged and his sense of fairness kept him on the hunt for new and better causes. Truth be known, Sam saw himself as a sort of minor superhero. Maybe not Super-man, but Reliable-man, or Dependa-man. Maybe Sir Justice, Protector of the Powerless, a name Kestrel had dubbed him with after her legal battles were done. Once he'd learned it was possible to help someone who'd been "done wrong," using the law degree he mostly got because his family insisted, he was always on the lookout for a cause. His dad ridiculed him at family holiday gatherings, but he thought maybe his siblings thought he was the tiniest bit noble. At least he hoped so.

Once he'd made the decision to be the best friend he could be to Kestrel, and nothing more, he was only slightly chagrined to realize that was exactly what Kestral had always thought he was.

San Francisco was a huge city for being so small. There was the usual complexity of caste, wealth, poverty, fairness, and cruel injustice. In her own little sphere, Kestrel watched, listened, and reported the stories of the wealthy and powerful. He wasn't sure why she focused her interests there, but she was good at it and got a thrill from bringing out the dark secrets she uncovered and shining the light on them. Last year she had nearly lost her life and her freedom when she'd uncovered some secrets that people were desperate not to have examined. Initially, there had just been some threats, but eventually it had landed her in hot water that required a lawyer. He knew she'd have gone to jail before she revealed her sources, but she didn't have to because she had Sam. Now, what she knew and how she knew it would come under scrutiny again. He hoped they'd be able to maintain her anonymity.

Fortunately, his latest project was at that in-between stage while the slow wheels of justice ground, weighed, and re-ground his months of work. He'd have the time and energy to be there for his neighbor if she needed him again.

CHAPTER TWENTY-NINE

Sunday, July 4 – Monday July 5

The wine had not kept Kestrel sleeping in and she'd awakened early, deciding to go to the farmer's market. Sunday mornings the street was blocked off and gardeners, bakers, beekeepers, knitters, canners, and various other artisans erected a dizzying display of pop-ups, tents, tables, racks, hooks, and poles to display their wares. She'd walked to the market carrying a string bag and her wallet and wearing a floppy hat. For once, she left her phone at home.

Surprisingly, the sun shone brightly on San Francisco this morning. Watching the people and cruising the offerings on display had lifted her spirits and she'd returned with an array of produce that she hoped only half of would die a lingering death in the back of the refrigerator before she gave up and threw it away. She was like her mother in more ways than one.

After she'd put the food away, she switched on her laptop and picked up her phone. Against her better judgment she checked her messages.

The clipped voice of Detective Raquel Stafford left a number for her to call and invited her to come down to the station to answer some additional questions and sign her statement, preferably on Monday. Kestrel noted the number and figured she could go and see what was up.

There were three messages from her mother in various states of chagrin over not being able to reach her. Kestrel figured Mom could wait. She supposed it would be her responsibility to tell her mother that Grace had been killed. Should she let the police do it? Would they even think to do it? They had, no doubt, already contacted Grace's adoptive parents and given them the bad news. She turned back to her computer. The last thing she needed was to get sidetracked envisioning that scene. She wondered if Bobby had been there.

She spent the afternoon putting finishing touches on the blog post of the week. It was engrossing to see how clearly you could identify well-known people and places without crossing the line into illegal territory. She called a couple of her contacts to confirm times and dates and zapped the missive out into cyberspace.

Monday morning Kestrel woke early for a shift at the PU Club. She delayed contacting Detective Stafford until later in the morning during her break. When she arrived at the police station for her two-p.m. appointment it took a few minutes for her to get up the courage to go in. The last time she had been there, she'd been under threat of being arrested, without much of a defense. She paced up and down a couple of times before approaching the desk.

"Um, I'm here to see Detective Stafford. My name is Kestrel Jonas."

"Yeah, just a second, I'll check in with her."

The desk sergeant dialed the extension, then left a message for Rocky.

"Just sit down over there. I'm sure Detective Stafford will get back to me right away."

Kestrel took a seat, then looked around. She always hated sitting here in the general population. Who the hell were these people, for crying out loud? She wondered if they were thinking the same about her.

The lyrics to Arlo Guthrie's "Alice's Restaurant Massacree" popped unbidden into her head. *"There was all kinds of mean, nasty, ugly-lookin' people on the bench there."* She hummed the tune under her breath.

After about fifteen minutes, the sergeant motioned her over to the desk. "Detective Stafford will meet you in the cafeteria in ten minutes."

Rocky did not usually meet people in the cafeteria. She had given some thought to the best way to get through Kestrel's defenses and figured she'd seen her share of ratty police office spaces. She had spent a lot of time following up on Kestrel's history with the department. She figured the woman didn't want to spend any more time here than absolutely necessary.

When Rocky entered the cafeteria, it took her a minute to identify Kestrel. Rocky's first impression had been that the waitress was a run-of-the-mill nobody. One of the legions of nondescript worker bees that staffed the myriad restaurants, hotels, clubs, and bars of San Francisco. But today Kestrel had decided to come as herself. Her tumble of hair fell below her shoulders and she was carefully made up. The black-rimmed glasses had disappeared, and the sweater, leggings and stylish boots revealed a surprisingly good figure. Maybe Bobby Burns wasn't such a moron, after all.

Rocky got a cup of coffee and approached the table where Kestrel played on her phone while flirting with the two officers at the next table.

"Ms. Jonas, thank you for coming." Rocky sat down.

"I just want to get all of this taken care of and get on with my life. Have you got the statement?"

"Yes, I do, and we appreciate you giving us access to your Heritage account. With your information we were able to contact the company and tie down some of the loose ends regarding Ms. Callahan's family."

"Have you got any more information about who might have killed her?"

"I wouldn't say we have gotten that far, but we are narrowing down who didn't commit the murder." Rocky took a sip of her coffee. "We have interviewed the half-brother she contacted. Um, if I understand how this DNA thing works, that would be your half-brother, as well."

"Yeah, I guess. Unless he killed her I am not very interested. So far, this relative thing hasn't worked out that well for me, or for Grace." Kestrel laughed nervously.

"I can't deny that. You know, he's here now."

"Here?" Kestrel glanced around the room.

"Not exactly here, but in the building. He's here to sign his statement, as well."

When Kestrel didn't say anything, Rocky couldn't help asking "Don't you want to meet him?"

Kestrel started. "Why would I want to meet him? He's nothing to me."

"Well, I'd want to at least know who he is if I were you."

"I guess I am a little curious. Could I just see him without talking to him? I really don't have anything to say to him."

Rocky considered this request for a moment. "I don't see why not. Get rid of your coffee and follow me. I think we can catch a glimpse."

Rocky knew exactly where to find Gari Graham, as she had just left him reading his typed statement for signature.

This building did not hold a lot of happy memories for Kestrel, except maybe that first kiss she and Bobby had shared in the stairwell down the hall from the bullpen. Other than that, it represented long hours of suspicion and interrogation, anger and animosity, accusations and denials.

The elevator stopped on the third floor and they walked to a door marked "Homicide."

Rocky opened the door and motioned for Kestrel to step inside. Once she'd closed the door, she motioned her head toward a desk on the other side of the room where Gari sat in one of the utilitarian side chairs talking to an officer. "There he is."

"That's not him."

"How do you know it's not him?"

"Because Grace described him to me and that is not who she described. Besides, I know that guy. Hell, everyone knows that guy."

"Well, according to Heritage and to Mr. Graham, he is the relative that was contacted by Ms. Callahan."

"That is not the guy she had dinner with. She told me about it and that is not him."

"Mr. Graham did not mention telling anyone else about having a sister."

"I don't care what he said. I do want to talk to him." Kestrel moved toward the seated figure but Rocky caught her arm.

"Not here, let me take you to a conference room and bring him in."

Kestrel looked skeptical. "It doesn't matter if he won't talk to me. I know where to find him whenever I want to."

"Okay, that's fine. But you should talk to him in private."

"Can I talk to him alone, without tapes or anything? I just want to know what is going on."

Rocky considered this for a moment. She probably shouldn't, but she hoped she could trust Kestrel to be honest with her.

"Okay, I will introduce you and leave you alone for a few minutes. But…" She paused speculatively. "You have got to tell me if he says anything of importance regarding this case."

Kestrel nodded in agreement as they reached the door of what, for lack of a better word, might be considered an interrogation room and Rocky left her there.

She wandered to the mirror on the side of the room and wondered whether there were people observing her from the other side. She made a funny face, or two, and then turned and sat with her back to the mirror.

It only took a few minutes for Rocky to return with Gari Graham in tow. She let him precede her into the room and then closed the door behind her. Gari looked a bit confused, but Rocky ended the confusion quickly.

"Mr. Graham, I wanted to take a moment to introduce you someone you should meet. This is Ms. Jonas, your sister."

"I thought you said she was murdered." He stammered.

"Oh, that was your other sister, Ms. Callahan." Rocky looked at her watch. "Wow, I've got to be someplace in about ten seconds. I'm sure you two have tons to talk about." With that she left the room.

After a few seconds Gari reached out to shake Kestrel's hand. "I'm happy to meet you. But I'm not sure what is going on here."

"Why don't you sit down, Mr. Graham, and I will clarify the sordid details for you."

Not knowing what else to do, Gari sat.

In as few words as possible, Kestrel laid out the general relationships between Gari, Grace, and herself. When she was done, she sat back and folded her arms, watching Gari carefully to see his reaction.

"Well, you can imagine this is quite a shock, Ms. Jones, is it?"

"Jonas," Kestrel corrected.

"Ms. Jonas. Sorry. You can imagine how much of a shock this is to me. I'm not sure what to say."

"I just want to know who you talked to about Grace contacting you."

"Nobody, really. I haven't even talked to my sisters about it. I was completely taken aback to be contacted by the police and I've given them all the information I have."

"That is not exactly true. Grace met someone, had dinner with someone, who said he was her brother. I want to know who it was."

"Honestly, I only spoke briefly with my attorney. You can imagine I didn't want to spread the story all over the city."

Kestrel almost laughed. No way was this staying a secret.

Gari had been agitated when the police contacted him and identified a murdered woman as the sister who had contacted him online. By the time he'd given his statement, and his airtight alibi for the time of the murder, he had felt more confident that it was all a ridiculous coincidence. Nobody in their right mind would think he could murder someone he didn't even know. He'd been pretty straightforward, but he didn't want to show all his cards until he'd had a chance to talk to George. George would know what was going on. Maybe Grace had told someone about the money from Gari and had been killed for it. Nobody had mentioned any money at her apartment, and he hadn't had the courage to ask. Now, there was this other sister, and she didn't look to be the kind who would take a payoff and fade into the shadows. "Don't I know you from somewhere? You look vaguely familiar."

"No, you don't know me, but I know you very well. I know your kind."

Gari started to object, but at that moment Rocky re-entered the room.

"So, how are you two getting along?" she asked cheerfully.

Kestrel stood up. "Oh, we are great pals already, aren't we, Gari?"

Gari didn't respond, but he didn't look as confident as he had when he had entered the room.

"Are we done here? I've signed my statement and I have nothing else to say. I assume I am free to go."

"Oh, sure, you can leave right now, Mr. Graham. I want to talk to Ms. Jonas for just a bit longer."

Gari was not accustomed to being dismissed, and really didn't like the idea of the two of them talking behind his back, but he couldn't think of a good reason to stay. He stood abruptly and left, letting the door slam shut behind him.

"Well, that must have been an interesting conversation."

"Yes, and no. He didn't really say much. Can you share his statement with me so I know where he is coming from?"

"Not really, but I can tell you he has a solid alibi, and you are the one who told me he did not match the victim's description of who she met with."

"No, he doesn't. But someone met with her and gave her the creeps."

"Any ideas?"

For a moment Rocky thought Kestrel might have more to say, but she just shook her head and looked away. "Do you still want me to sign my statement? I have to work at The Towers later."

Rocky would have liked to press the matter. Something was going on behind those intelligent eyes. Instead, she escorted Kestrel to her desk to review and sign the statement.

CHAPTER THIRTY

Tuesday, July 6

For Gari Graham, the day was fraught with anxiety. He was new to the idea of sisters popping out of the woodwork and the possibility he was connected in some obscure way with the death of a woman he'd never met. After meeting Kestrel at the police station on Monday afternoon, he'd frantically tried to reach George at his office, but he was out. The home phone went to voicemail, and his cell phone was turned off and his voicemail box full. Gari knew Amélie and the kids were with his own wife and kids on the coast, some mother/child yoga bonding BS that cost more than they paid the housekeeper in six months.

He'd finally downed enough scotch to knock himself out, and almost missed the chirpy morning phone call from Mary the next day. What was it with video calling? She looked like hell and the grinning faces of his children blown up on the phone screen were definitely not what he wanted to see after the night he'd had. His calls to George began again early on Tuesday after a restless night.

***

Amélie and Mary, on the other hand, had slept like logs. This morning had found them sipping mimosas as they kissed the kids off to the Zen master in charge. Did it matter, really, if the actual week was yoga for kids, where parents were asked to distance themselves from the grounding of their children, preferably by fabulous bag shopping at the Coach outlet, a wonderful lunch in Carmel, and enough booze to sink numerous ships.

Mary and Amélie were not particularly close. Amélie, being one of the elite Graham clan, had experienced all of the perks of familial wealth. Mary, on the other hand, had been second-tier wealthy in San Francisco, but had accomplished a coup by a marriage into the upper ranks. She was much prettier and more talented than her sister-in-law, and her deb year had been quite the event. Of course, now that it was not politically correct to have a coming-out ball, it was a definite benefit to be both beautiful and smart. Her capture of Gari Graham's interest and hand reminded her of the line in *Sense and Sensibility* where Mr. Ferrars' sister says that she wouldn't be surprised if Lucy Steele married far beyond her expectations. Marriage to Gari had been surprisingly beneficial. He was a fairly nice person, not too demanding, and considered himself blessed by his marriage to Mary, the beautiful children they had produced, and her meaningful and well-intended contribution to San Francisco and his family reputation, in general.

Up until the debacle produced by his father's death and disturbing legacy, their marriage had been as good any she knew.

Amélie, on the other hand, had probably undervalued herself and her marriage to George Musgrove may have been ill-advised. The years had shown her that she had far more to offer to the world and to her family than she had originally thought. George did not have the pedigree, but he was charming and there was a magnetism about him that drew her, even when she found his crass behavior and base background an embarrassment.

CHAPTER THIRTY-ONE

Tuesday, July 6

When George woke up on Tuesday he was greeted by a dozen urgent phone messages from Gari. He'd shut off both his cell phone and the home line just to get some sleep. He was just having his first peaceful cup of coffee and checking his phone when it rang again and George picked it up. He took a deep breath before he answered.

"Hey, Gari, how are you?"

"I am not good, George. Not good at all. I need to see you right away."

"What's going on, man?" George was surprised by the alarm in Gari's voice.

"I can't tell you on the phone. I need to see you."

"What's the matter with you, just calm down." George could feel the tension in his own voice.

"That girl, Grace, she's dead and the police have been asking me questions. They know she was in touch with me, they think I met with her. There are two of them, George."

"Two of who, Gari, you're not making any sense."

"Two sisters, and one of them is dead and the other one was at the police station."

"Fuck." George couldn't think of what else to say. "Okay, I can meet you later at that bar we used to go to in school. The tacky one near the baseball park."

"I'll be there at two."

"Fine." George clicked out of the call and swiveled his chair so that he was looking out over the city. He just had to get his story straight with Gari.

***

George's dark Mercedes slid quietly out of the garage and headed south toward Tommy's Joynt on Geary Boulevard. Traffic was heavy and Kestrel's ancient Volkswagen, singularly inconspicuous for its blandness, followed along behind him. She had realized that Grace's description of the brother she'd met, perfectly described Gari's friend from the Pacific Union Club.

It had been easy for Kestrel to call George's office and find out he wasn't in, so she'd gone directly to his home address.

It was no problem to tail George as he meandered through the streets. He pulled into a parking lot on Geary and she drove right past and circled the block, pulling into the same lot in time to follow him down the street to a bar. She had reverted to her work disguise and ordered a burger to go at the counter. While she feigned interest in the posters on the wall, she used her phone to snap several pictures of George and Gari talking intensely at a corner table. When she got outside she took the time to text the picture to Rocky with the note, "This is the guy I think Grace met with."

As she stepped out onto the street, she placed a quick call to an old friend and contact, Lester Stuyvesant, aspiring actor and private detective. It went straight to voicemail and she left a message for an urgent call back.

***

George had never seen Gari so agitated. When he first entered the dim restaurant, he spotted Gari right away. Gari had been anxiously watching the door and almost leapt to his feet when he saw George.

Gari leaned across the table as soon as George sat down.

"What the hell have you gotten me into?" he whispered.

"Relax, Gari, you're drawing attention to yourself."

Gari leaned back a bit but he was still tense.

"George, the police called me at the house this morning and asked me to come down to the station. I couldn't even imagine what it was about and then they said it was a homicide investigation. Murder, George!"

"Wait a minute. Don't get all rattled. We didn't do anything to that girl. How did they even get your name?"

"There's another sister who told them about the Heritage thing and said that I had met with the dead girl. Did you give her my name, you moron?"

"Of course, I didn't. They must have gone to Heritage to get your info. Just relax! They can't prove you ever met with her. You're fine." George sounded a lot calmer than he was. Holy shit! Once they had contacted Gari it was a slam dunk they would connect him to this.

"Did you tell them I met with her?"

"No, I didn't tell them anything except I'd gotten an email. They already had that. I didn't want to say anything until I talked to you to find out what was going on. What *is* going on, George? What did you do?"

Gari's voice had started to rise and George glanced around the room. "I did what I told you I was going to do. I gave her the money. Lower your voice."

"Shit, the money. That is going to look great to the cops. Some girl contacts me, I give her a ton of money and then she's killed."

"That's probably why she was killed. We don't know her, who she told about the money. Did they find the money on her?"

"How would I know? I didn't ask if she had a ton of cash on her."

"Relax. Let me get us a beer and you can tell me what they said."

George went to the bar. He was so rattled he stood for several minutes staring at the international beer menu before he ordered two domestic lights. The first thing he needed Gari to do was settle down and then he needed to figure out how he'd been linked to this. He thought he'd been sly. No links, no evidence, no witnesses. He needed to figure out how to spin his story.

By the time George returned with the beers Gari had calmed down a bit, but still looked like he could spin out of control any second.

"So, tell me exactly what the police said."

Gari took a steadying breath. "They told me that a young woman had been murdered and that I might know her. I couldn't even think who they might mean. They told me her name was Grace Callahan and I said I had never heard of her. Then the detective said that was strange since they had an email from her telling me she was my sister. Christ, it didn't have her name on it, it came through with a code or initials or something. I don't even remember."

"Okay, that's good. That's understandable that you wouldn't recognize the name."

"So, then they tell me that her computer and phone were missing but someone told them that I met with her. Had dinner with her."

"Yes, you know that I went to meet her. I told her I was her brother, but I gave her a fake name, not yours or mine. She couldn't have told anyone that."

"Yeah, but she did tell someone about the meeting. Her sister, my sister!"

"She never said anything about a sister."

"I can't help that, George. There is a sister and she was there."

"She was where, at the murder?"

"No, asshole, at the police station."

George took a long drink of his beer to give him a chance to think.

"How do you know she was at the station?"

"Because I met her. They stuck me in an interrogation room and this woman was there, and she told me that she was my sister."

"Okay, but that still doesn't have anything to do with us. Just because your dad was out there dropping bastards, doesn't mean we did anything wrong. Maybe the sister killed her for the money. When was she murdered?"

"Thursday night. It was Thursday night because they asked me where I was."

"And you had an alibi, right? Where did you tell them you were?"

"We were at the fund-raiser for the school. We were there all evening and then we went home. Probably fifty people saw me there until eleven-thirty. You missed it. Where were you, anyway?"

"That was our opera night, so I have an alibi, as well. Hundreds of people saw me." George was a bit miffed that Gari would ask him for an alibi, but then, that was why he had manufactured such an elaborate one.

George finished his beer and glanced at his watch. "Just relax. It is just a coincidence that the woman was killed after she contacted you. We both have foolproof alibis and there is no real connection to us, or to any money. Pull yourself together."

As they started out the door George turned to Gari. "What was the sister like, the live sister?"

"Just a woman. She looked kind of familiar, but she said we'd never met."

"She probably looked like your father and your other sisters. That would be familiar."

"Yeah, right. I guess so."

CHAPTER THIRTY-TWO

Tuesday, July 6

As Kestrel pulled away from the curb her cell phone began to ring. Not for the first time she wished she had a newer car with hands-free calling. At least on public transportation you could keep moving while you annoyed other riders with your calls.

She swerved to the curb in a bus-only spot and grabbed up the phone she'd tossed on the seat. It was Lester calling her back.

"Lester, thanks for returning my call."

"No problem, Kestrel. It's been a long time, but I don't have any new scoops for you."

"Not looking for scoops today. I have a job for you."

That got Lester's attention. He hadn't been working that much lately and his wardrobe change to "Game of Thrones"-mode had been costing him a lot of money. Today was warm and he was somewhat regretting his choice of that new leather jerkin over a puffy shirt. Going to a stylist for the longer hair cost a lot more than the old barber down the street. And product, damn, that stuff was expensive. "Okay, then. Do you want to meet and talk it over?"

"Where are you now? I'm just leaving Tommy's Joynt and there's someone there I want to have followed."

"Wow, okay. I guess I could be there in about fifteen minutes."

"He might still be there by then. You head that way and I'll send you a picture. There are two guys but I want you to follow the dark-haired one. If he's still there when you get there, just to follow him today to see where he goes. We can talk later and I'll fill you in. Right now I am running late for something and have to go."

"Okay, then. I'll head out now."

Before she pulled the VW back onto the street, just as a bus pulled into the spot, she sent the picture of Gari and George to Lester.

She hadn't driven a block when her phone rang again. Glancing down she saw it was Lester, but she didn't have time to stop again. She'd call him later.

When she got to her house to dump the car and head to The Towers she glanced at the text message Lester had sent. "I know this guy. I've followed him before. Call me!"

She messaged Lester she'd call later and hurried to make her shift.

It was late when Kestrel finally got home. There were three messages from Lester but rather than listen to them she decided to just call him. The hell with the time.

"Hello, who the hell calls at midnight?" Lester did not sound amused.

"If you read your caller ID you will see that it is me, answering your numerous calls."

"Yeah, yeah, I get it. I just have to tell you the guy went the same place he went the last time I followed him, to his house in Pacific Heights. My McDonald's drive-through of a Big Mac Meal, super-sized, will be on your bill."

"That all makes sense but what doesn't make sense is why you would have followed the same guy before."

"It was his wife, hoping to catch him cheating, I guess. But, not from what I saw. Had dinner with a much younger lady, talked, dropped her at her place on Fulton Street and went home to the wife and kiddies."

"On Fulton Street? Where exactly?"

"Just up from the opera house, 'round the corner from the 'painted ladies.'"

"I knew it! Goddamn, Lester, you are a fucking genius."

"You ain't tellin' me anything I don't know, but why did you want this guy followed? Is he cheating on you with his wife?"

"No, Lester, that girl he dropped off is dead now and she was my sister."

For once Lester was completely silent. It wasn't often he was taken off-guard, but this was a new one for him. "She's dead, you mean like in murdered?"

"Yes, like in murdered." Maybe Lester wasn't quite the genius she had given him credit for. "When did you follow him to her house?"

"Let me check my calendar. Here it is. It was Monday a week ago. I sent the report to the wife on Tuesday. She paid right away, by check in a couple of days."

"You still have the report? I need you to send a copy to me, can you email it?"

"Not sure if it's kosher to send a private report to someone."

"Fine, I'll pay you, but it isn't for me, it's for the police."

"Yikes, the police, that makes it worse. I'll tell you what. I will redact my name and send you a picture that you can send to them. If they are going to need to talk to me, I want a heads-up."

"That works; it is just part of the evidence I've come up with. Right now, it doesn't matter that much who saw him there, but it will at some point."

"Shit…"

"It could get your name in the paper, you super-sleuth, you." Kestrel gave the free publicity angle a minute to percolate through Lester's sleepy brain.

Lester sighed. "I'll send you the redacted report first thing in the morning."

"Not in the morning, I need it now."

"I will send it now if you promise to not call me again tonight. I'm bushed."

"You have a deal."

It took about ten minutes for Lester to do whatever he needed to do with the report and attach a picture of George and Grace at dinner, then her phone buzzed. Then it took about ten minutes more for her to save it someplace separate from his phone number and forward it on to Rocky Stafford with the cryptic note, "See report below, and picture, of George Musgrove seen with Grace Callahan."

Kestrel forwarded that photo to Detective Stafford, as well.

***

Rocky had just dozed off when her phone buzzed on the bedside table. She squinted at it, the bright screen hurting her eyes. "Well, damn." Whereupon she put the phone back down, turned over and went back to sleep. Things were starting to get interesting but there was nothing she could do until morning.

CHAPTER THIRTY-THREE

Wednesday, July 7

Detective Raquel Stafford stopped before entering the interrogation room to recheck the texts she'd received from Kestrel Jonas, recent witness and general pain in the ass. The attached picture showed two men: the suspect, Gari Graham, and another man who fit the description Kestrel had provided of the brother who met with Grace. Another picture showed a dark man and a young woman in a restaurant. Rocky wasn't sure what it all meant, but she would follow up after she'd questioned Grace's boyfriend, Kevin Durbin.

When she entered the room Kevin, who'd been lounging back in the chair, playing with his phone and grinning, sat up a little straighter and made his best effort to look bereaved.

"Kevin Durbin? I'm Detective Stafford, Homicide. I believe you have already been informed that your friend, Grace Callahan, was found murdered in her apartment a few days ago."

"Yes." Kevin had the good grace to look solemn and shook his head sadly.

Rocky sat down. She took a couple of minutes to open the file before her and glance through the statements and pictures.

"According to your statement and those of neighbors, you were possibly one of the last people to see Ms. Callahan on the evening she died. Is that correct?"

"I guess so." Kevin was a regular font of voluntary information.

Rocky tried again. "Why don't you tell me when you last saw her and what the two of you talked about."

"Umm, okay. It's all there in the statement. I kind of hate talking about it."

"I understand, but we want to make sure we have all the information and you might not have remembered to tell us some little thing that could help us find the perpetrator of this crime. You'd want to help as much as you can, wouldn't you?"

Kevin shifted uncomfortably in the chair. "Sure, I just don't remember much."

"That's fine. Just tell me, in your own words, what you do remember about that evening."

"Well, Grace and I were supposed to go out to dinner. To go up to see my Grammy at The Towers."

Rocky glanced down at the statement before her, "Did you go to dinner with your Grammy, um… Mrs. Lilah Durbin?"

"No, when I went to pick Grace up she was upset about something and said she didn't want to go, so we didn't."

Rocky shuffled the papers before her and pulled one out of the folder.

"According to one of Ms. Callahan's neighbors there was some shouting and you 'slammed out the door and down the stairs.' Is that correct?"

"I did kind of rush out and the door probably slammed. I told you Grace was upset about something."

"Do you know what she was upset about?"

"It had something to do with finding her real family."

"Why were you upset and shouting?"

"Well, it made me mad that she was embarrassing me in front of my grandmother."

Rocky looked down at the statement. "Says here that you shouted the words 'You fucking bitch, I don't need your shit in my life' as you were leaving."

"I know, I feel really badly that those were my last words to her. It just pissed me off that she was letting some bullshit thing that had nothing to do with me mess up my plans." Rocky would have had a little more sympathy if his voice hadn't carried that injured-white-boy whine that she hated so much.

"Where did you go when you left Ms. Callahan's home? Did you go to dinner at The Towers?"

"No, there was no point. The whole dinner was about my Grammy getting to see Grace. Grammy's not going to hang in there much longer and she just loves... loved, Grace. She was set on us getting married and wanted to make plans and set a date."

"Really, how did you and Grace feel about that?"

"I don't know if we were ready for marriage, but we were willing to talk to her about it. Look, I have not been close with Grammy in a while. She didn't approve of me and I didn't really care. But I'm her only grandchild and, with Grace in the picture, she hoped we'd get married and carry on the family name and all that."

"Have you told her that Ms. Callahan is dead?"

"No, and I'm not going to. She's sick and she'll probably die soon. What good would it do to make her unhappy?"

Rocky wondered how sick Grammy was and how soon she was expected to die off but decided to set aside those questions for a bit.

Just at that moment the door opened and Detective Bobby Burns sidestepped into the room, shutting the door quietly behind him.

"Mr. Durbin, this is Detective Burns. He'll be joining me and may have a few questions of his own."

Kevin nodded at Bobby and angled his body more in the male detective's direction, the preference for talking to a man being obvious in the movement.

Rocky resumed her questioning but had to wait a moment for Kevin to reluctantly shift his attention back to her.

"If you did not go to The Towers for dinner with your grandmother, where did you go after leaving Ms. Callahan's home?"

"I called a friend and we went to Specs to have a few drinks and relax."

"Specs?"

Bobby spoke up. "It's a club in the Castro. You've seen it. It used to be a church and the cross is still up on the steeple. Specs is short for Spectacles, Testicles, Wallet and Watch."

When Rocky still looked confused Kevin chimed in, "You know, like in *Austin Powers*."

"Never mind, Detective, you can check it out on YouTube. It's just an inside joke–reference," Bobby contributed.

Rocky eyed Bobby speculatively, wondering how he was so familiar with the Castro District of San Francisco, and inside jokes having to do with whoever this Austin Powers person was.

"By the way, you might want to let your grandmother know about Ms. Callahan's death. We may need to talk to her about your dinner plans, and the bad news would be better coming from you."

She finished up the interview and asked Kevin Durbin to come back and sign the statement when it had been completed.

Outside the interrogation room she eyed Bobby Burns speculatively. "How do you know so much about this 'Specs' club?"

"I don't know much about it. I just know what it is."

"Okay, but how would you know that stuff?"

"Listen, Detective Stafford, San Francisco is not just any city. You need to know who you are dealing with and where they stand."

For a moment Rocky Stafford considered that Los Angeles or Oakland might be a little bit easier to categorize.

Rocky pulled out her cell phone. "By the way, I have messages and photos from your girlfriend, the investigative reporter-slash-waitress." She held up the phone for Bobby to see the messages and photos Kestrel had sent. "Looks like she's doing a little stakeout of her own."

***

Bobby was alarmed that Kestrel was snooping around again. She had a penchant for getting herself into deep trouble without meaning to. He only said, "She's not my girlfriend."

CHAPTER THIRTY-FOUR

Wednesday, July 7

Kevin checked in at the front desk of The Towers and waited while the receptionist called to let Lilah Durbin know her grandson was on the way up.

He stood outside the door of her apartment before knocking. Finally, he took a deep breath and rapped on the door. Lilah answered almost immediately. "Kevin, I'm so surprised to see you." Seeing the expression on his face she faltered in her greeting. "What's wrong Kevin, what is it?"

"Oh my God, Grammy, I have some terrible news."

"Come in, come in, what is it?" She tried to put her arms around him, but he shrugged her away and walked past her.

"I think you need to sit down. This is terrible news."

Lilah looked confused but obeyed his request and sat on the edge of the sofa. "What is it, Kevin, what is going on?"

He sat down on the hassock across from her and took her hands in his. "Grammy, I have to tell you that Grace has been killed. She's gone."

For several seconds Lilah did not seem to register what he had said.

"Grace has been killed" was such an unexpected announcement. "What do you mean; was it an accident?"

"It was murder, Grammy, and I think the police think I may have done it." Kevin looked suitably ravaged, but it was hard to tell whether it was grief or anxiety.

"Of course they don't think it was you. Tell me what happened."

Inside Lilah there was a struggle to decide whether to be horrified at Grace's death or supportive of her only grandchild. For the moment Lilah put aside the choice and gripped Kevin's hands as he sat down beside her.

"I wasn't going to tell you because I know how much you cared about her, but then the police brought me down to the station and asked a lot of questions. They may come here to find out about me and Grace, to ask about our dinner plans on Thursday."

"Oh my God, was that when she was killed?"

"Yes, someone came to her apartment after I left her and they killed her, took her phone and computer. I didn't even find out about it until Saturday."

"That poor girl." Lilah didn't know what to say. She'd had such high hopes for Kevin and for Grace, for her family. She'd never known anyone who'd been murdered before, but of course, Kevin couldn't have done it. What were the police thinking?

They sat in silence for a bit before Lilah pulled herself together. "I was just about to go down to dinner, why don't you go with me? Just let me get a sweater, they keep it kind of cool in the dining room. I'll pick out a nice bottle of wine for us to take down, as well."

Lilah rose and walked into the bedroom and Kevin walked over to the display case in the entry. His gaze fell on a small figurine of a mermaid. He had not seen it before but was drawn to the sparkle of it. Lilah didn't buy crap and he couldn't help thinking of Sweetpea and her penchant for mermaids. Picking it up, he noted it was heavier than expected, probably gold. He shrugged and slipped it into his pocket right before Lilah re-entered the room. She walked toward him and gazed pointedly at the empty space on the shelf. Kevin would have rearranged the knick-knacks to cover the space if he'd had time. He wondered if she would mention the missing item, but she turned toward the door with a sigh of resignation. He was home safe, again.

Kestrel was working the dining room when she saw Lilah enter with her grandson. The older woman moved slowly to one of the smaller tables without stopping to speak to her various acquaintances already seated for dinner.

When Kestrel came to their table, she saw that Lilah had been crying. "Are you all right, Mrs. Durbin?"

Looking up, Lilah clutched Kestrel's hand. "Oh, Kay, my dear boy's fiancée has been killed… murdered." The word hung in the air for a moment. "Poor, poor Grace."

A shock went through Kestrel's body at those words. Kevin, Grace, murder! It couldn't be that his Grace and her Grace were the same person. She turned to him sharply. She had seen him before in this room with his family, but she had also seen him in that smiling ski picture on Grace's bookshelf. He was the shitty boyfriend and the shitty grandson. "I'm so sorry, Mrs. Durbin. Can I get you anything?"

"Yes, dear, some ice water and we'll need wineglasses and this bottle opened." Lilah reached out and patted Kevin's arm as Kestrel turned and walked out of the dining room. She stopped long enough to give one of the other staff the instructions and the bottle of wine and then went to the restroom and locked herself in a stall.

She needed a few minutes to think. To compose herself. Had Grace really been the fiancée she had seen just a few weeks ago at dinner? Was the man with Lilah Durbin her dead sister's boyfriend? The woman she'd seen at dinner had looked familiar, but she hadn't met Grace then, hadn't made the connection.

How could that be true? She didn't know Kevin Durbin, but she knew of him. His bad-boy reputation, the way his grandmother spoke of him, what Grace had said to her that only time they met.

The minutes ticked by and after a bit, K. Jones left the stall, splashed some cold water on her face, and went to find her manager. The dining room was slow tonight and the service was nearly over. When she found her boss, her face was pale and her hands trembled. There was no problem convincing him she needed to leave early. She hesitated over whether to say good-bye to Lilah but didn't know what she could say. She was certainly not going to insert her own story into the drama being played out between Lilah and her grandson.

Looking back, Kestrel would not remember standing at the bus stop as wisps of fog swirled around her, the sticky surface of the cracked seats on the bus, or automatically getting off at her regular stop and walking up the hill to her home. She stood for a moment on the doorstep and gazed through the dark apartment window before she stepped to the right and knocked on Sam's door.

The jazzy music he liked to listen to when he relaxed seeped dreamily through the slightly open window of the kitchen along with the seductive scent of garlic and tomatoes. There was a dim light coming from farther into the apartment, but in a few moments his substantial bulk blocked the light as he answered the door. "Kestrel, hey."

"Hey, Sam." Now that he had answered she wasn't sure what she needed to say. "Look, I've had a God-awful day and need some food and wine… maybe a lot of wine."

As he always had, he stepped back from the door so that she could enter. Sam had been the shelter, the respite, the soft shoulder to cry on ever since they had decided to remain friends rather than become lovers. If she'd had a brother, she'd have wished it were Sam. Wait, she had a brother and he was an entitled asshole to the best of her knowledge. She preferred Sam.

The guy was brilliant, and educated, and a total pushover for a noble cause. They'd shared many bottles of wine and a few soft kisses and fumbling gropes, but nothing had ever really developed. Why couldn't she go for nice solid guys like Sam? Why did she have to hanker after edgy, sketchy, elusive bad boys?

She proceeded into the living/dining room of the apartment. It was just like hers but turned around in that disorienting way of duplexes. His was cleaner, and messier. The furniture glowed with wax and there were no cobwebs and fuzz balls lurking under his dining table. But the table was piled with file folders and law books. He worked as an attorney, but his goal was justice, which often had nothing at all to do with the court system. The cases he took outside his law offices supported his true passion, helping the wrongly convicted. One time she had figured out that the hours spent at his "job" were about half as many as the hours he spent here poring over court documents, law tomes, and evidence. At the time she thought it was a fool's game, but she'd been incredibly grateful for his help when her own ass was on the line over accidentally uncovered graft at the highest level of San Francisco government. She'd probably have slept with him based only on gratitude, but Sam deserved so much more than that. In the end they both realized he was the big brother she, and everyone else, should have had.

Tonight, he didn't ask a lot of questions. He poured some wine, dished up some of his epic lasagna, and let her wallow for a bit in the warmth and familiarity of his home.

"It's completely insane," Kestrel slurred at some point. "I didn't know her at all. I have gossip sources I know more about. But I thought we'd have time to get sick of each other, to hate what the other one thought, but still love them, just because."

At some point Kestrel's tears overcame her rambling conversation and Sam let her just lean against him with his arm around her.

Kestrel surfaced groggily from a scattered dream. It started with the swell of recognition and joy she'd felt when she saw Grace in the lobby of the Academy of Sciences, proceeded to her recognition of the brother Grace had described, and faded into a murky scene where she and Lilah Durbin stood together in the dining room of The Towers and looked down on Grace's body.

Kestrel realized that she lay on the sofa of Sam's apartment. He'd carefully spread a blanket over her and had spent the night safely ensconced in his pristine bedroom. It took a few minutes for Kestrel to realize where she was, and once again, to realize that Sam was too good a guy to take advantage of her in spite of her diminished emotional status.

How many times had she been in his apartment, drunk and available, and found herself hungover and unravished on his sofa? She smelled coffee from the kitchen, but when she staggered in, found that he was behind his closed bedroom door, leaving the freshly ground, French-pressed, and ready-to-pour coffee on the counter.

She opened the refrigerator realizing his was as poorly stocked as her own. She closed the door and sat down at the kitchen table.

The strange dream still drifted around the edges of her consciousness and she tried to think who would want to kill Grace, and why. Was her death one of the seemingly random acts of greed and need that killed so many? Was she just in the wrong place at the wrong time? Why did it coincide with finding family; who would gain or lose? Kestrel felt the beginning of the tickle that so often told her something was up that she didn't yet see. Who were the people in Grace's life, and what did Kestrel know about them? Kevin, her boyfriend, grandson of a wealthy woman. Gari Graham, a brother she had just discovered, and his weaselly lawyer friend who had represented himself to Grace as her brother but given a fake name and history, who had offered Grace money to disappear. Two fortunes were at stake here. The challenge to Garrett Graham's estate, left to charities, which was likely being decided in the courts at this very moment. What did the appearance of Grace Callahan mean to that court case? For that matter, what did her own relationship to the Graham family mean? What about Lilah Durbin: wealthy, aging, and estranged from her only grandson until Grace came into the picture? Who could benefit from Grace's death, the Graham family? It would seem that Kevin was better off with Grace in the picture, but she'd heard the uncertainty in Grace's voice when she spoke of him.

Kestrel's blog research had made her familiar with the Grahams and with Lilah's history, but she didn't know much about Kevin, other than being a tribulation to his grandmother. Maybe it was time to check him out.

Finishing her coffee, she rinsed the cup and left it in the drainer by the sink.

"Bye, Sam, thanks for food and wine… and the coffee," she called as she let herself out the kitchen door and returned to her own apartment.

CHAPTER THIRTY-FIVE

Thursday, July 8

George had not slept well. The revelations from Gari had spiraled around in his scotch-soaked brain most of the night and he'd finally fallen into a stuporous sleep right before sunrise.

At eight-fifteen his phone rang. It was work calling and he let it go to voicemail. Ten minutes later it rang again, and then ten minutes after that. Finally, he picked it up. "Connie, what could be so goddamned important you have to call me on my day off?"

There was a pause before a deep voice that was definitely not his admin, Connie, responded. "This is Dixon, George."

"Dixon… sorry, I just woke up. What can I do for you, man?"

"I want to meet with you this morning. Will ten o'clock work?" It wasn't really a question, and George knew it.

"Sure, I can do that. What's up?"

"Just something I need you to do for me, right away."

"Okay, well, see you then."

"Yes." The dial tone signaled that, as far as Dixon was concerned, the call was over.

In the shower George speculated on what Dixon could want. They didn't usually have a lot to do with each other and that suited both of them just fine. It was probably nothing important. George categorized Dixon in that privileged class that thought their every whim was urgent. Oh, well, couldn't hurt to make some points with the boss.

George arrived promptly at ten and went directly to Dixon's office. Instead of the usual admin announcement and de rigueur wait he was directed to go right in.

"Here are some papers I need signed by a client in the North Bay." Never one to waste time Dixon brandished the manila envelope in George's direction, not even inviting him to sit down.

George didn't take them right away. What was this anyway? A paralegal or a courier could take papers across the Golden Gate in the horrendous traffic. "I am actually off this week for a few days of R and R."

Since Dixon didn't lower his arm George eventually reached out and took the envelope.

"Victoria McKenzie" was neatly typed on the label with an address in Sausalito.

"So, who is Victoria McKenzie?"

"This is sensitive, but minor. This woman has been receiving, let's say a retainer, from the Graham Trust for many years. We thought it had been finalized but we've heard from her again recently."

"That doesn't tell me who she is." He was still stung by being made the designated errand boy.

"Does it matter, George? Garrett Graham screwed up a generation ago and has been paying for it ever since. Victoria is just the manifestation of one of his many nightmares. His baby mama if you will." You could hear the disdain in Dixon's voice but George couldn't tell if it was for Victoria or for Garrett, Senior.

"So, what, I just go get these signed?"

"Pretty much, but there is a check there, too. That gets left behind. If we can get the trust debacle settled soon it should be the last one."

George had been watching Dixon closely. Here was another piece of the puzzle. He was busy calculating how he could benefit from this new piece of information. Victoria was the mother; Grace was, had been, the child. Dixon didn't act like he had heard about Grace contacting Gari, or anything after that. It was clear Gari hadn't known about Victoria. The question was, how much of a threat was she to the family inheritance? Did she have a claim?

Not knowing what else to do, and intensely curious, George had taken the papers from Dixon and headed across the Golden Gate.

Victoria had not been what he expected. Smaller, younger- looking, and very much not alone. She answered his knock wrapped scantily in a red silk kimono and the cloud of cannabis smoke and incense wafted over him. He gave her his card and she motioned him into the kitchen. A large naked man walked out of what was likely the bedroom, opened the fridge, and pulled out a chilled bottle of champagne. "Bubbly?" he said to George, motioning with the bottle.

"No, thanks."

Victoria sat down at the table and her wrap opened carelessly. "You have something for me to sign?"

George pulled the papers out of the envelope and the check slipped out and fell to the floor.

"Sign at each of the places tagged on the document, and initial at the bottom of each page." He handed her his pen.

While she signed, he bent down and picked up the check, $250,000. He knew that was just a drop in the Garrett fortune, but still, you'd think she would be excited, or grateful, or maybe slightly embarrassed, but she wasn't. She was annoyed at being interrupted and anxious to sign the papers and get rid of him.

The whole interaction had taken less than ten minutes and George had been summarily dismissed.

***

Kestrel had one of her rare days off, and yet again, here she was, headed for her mother's house. Victoria had left several plaintive messages this week and it seemed it might be a good idea to swing by the house in Marin to see what was up. Besides, there was the issue of telling her about Grace.

Just as Kestrel steered the VW onto the dusty road to her mother's house, she spotted a dark BMW turning onto the main road, and at the wheel sat George. He didn't look her way. In fact, if she hadn't been turning, he'd have pulled out right in front of her.

Kestrel's heart dropped. What was George doing here? She sped down the lane and parked in her accustomed spot behind the hedge. She could see that Victoria's car was there and she hurried to the door.

The door stood slightly ajar and she could hear the strains of New Age music in the background. Pushing the door open she caught a whiff of patchouli incense and marijuana smoke. She stepped carefully into the living room and saw that her mother's bedroom door was open. Kestrel tiptoed across the room. She felt silly being so stealthy, but was tentative about what she might find.

She could see the waver of candlelight on the dim walls as she peeked around the door.

Victoria lay naked on the floor in a circle of lit candles, her long hair spread out around her head. What kind of sick weirdo was George Musgrove, anyway? She rushed into the room and fell on her knees next to the still form. "Oh my God, Mom, Mom!"

Victoria shrieked and sat bolt upright, pushing Kestrel away from herself. "Kestrel, what are you doing here? You scared me to death!"

"I thought you were dead. What are you doing?"

"I'm waiting for Armand. We're *trying* to have Tantric sex, but he had to pee first."

Kestrel took a deep breath just as the bathroom door opened and a very naked, noticeably young man stepped into the bedroom. "What's up, Victoria?"

"Nothing, Armie, it's just my daugh—um, friend, Kestrel, being a maniac, as usual." It wouldn't do to have her latest lover realize she had a daughter about his same age.

Apparently, neither Victoria nor Armand thought anything of their nakedness and it was Kestrel who looked away, embarrassed.

Victoria rose from the floor and walked over to the bedside table where a pipe of probably supreme-grade marijuana still burned. She picked it up and took a long toke. She held the smoke in expertly and closed her eyes for several seconds. She didn't speak until she had released the smoke. "Honestly, between you and that damned attorney I am completely losing the mood."

"There was an attorney here?"

"Yeah, some guy wanting to have some papers signed for a, um...

financial transaction I am involved in." Kestrel could see Victoria glance away as she said this.

Things were falling into place for Kestrel. First finding out Gari was her brother, which made the late Garrett Graham her father, *and* Grace's father. This was about money, for Victoria. That was all it was about for her. George hadn't been there to kill Victoria; he'd been there to buy her off. For a moment Kestrel could have killed her mother herself if Armand hadn't been standing there in all his nakedness, eyeing them both speculatively.

"You don't have to hide this shit from me, Mom. I know Garrett Graham was my father and that little prick who interrupted your foreplay was his attorney."

"What difference does it make to you? None of it is any of your business. How do you know that, anyway?"

"I know that because I met my dear brother at the police station. Somebody murdered Grace and it didn't take them long to connect the DNA dots. You should have seen Gari Graham's face when he met his dear sister."

It was almost worth the drama to see the shocked look on Victoria's face. She took another long toke from the pipe and released it before speaking.

"Well, hell. I ought to sue those damned Heritage people. What a cock-up."

***

The traffic was not as heavy headed back into the city and George had a chance to reflect. Amélie had not mentioned wanting a divorce again and George had been on good behavior. If he worked it right, he could head off the inevitable and maintain the extra money and the lifestyle. If not, he was not above suing for custody of the kids and strong-arming child support and alimony out of his wife. He knew Amélie well and he knew she would never have dumped him if she didn't have someone suitable waiting in the wings. He didn't really care, although he wondered who it might be. It would just be another piece of leverage in the divorce if it were true.

CHAPTER THIRTY-SIX

Thursday, July 8

Rocky and Bobby entered the darkened club trying not to look too obviously official. It was lunchtime, and the way that heads went up in the room and elbows prodded those who hadn't seen, they knew there was no point in pretending they weren't police.

Rocky made her way to the bar, threading through the scattered tables. The bartender smiled. "Officer, how can I help you?"

"Detectives Stafford and Burns. We just have a couple of questions about someone who is using your establishment for an alibi." Rocky flipped open her identification and the barkeep's eyes widened a bit.

"Wow, Homicide. Not our usual investigations."

"Really, what are your usual investigations?"

"Oh, you know, lewd and indecent behavior, public nudity, child endangerment."

The server clearing tables behind them snickered and then quickly walked away after receiving an unamused glance from Rocky.

"One of our witnesses indicated that he was here all evening on Thursday. Could you look at this picture and tell me if you have ever seen this person in the bar?"

Bobby pulled out a picture of Kevin. It was one they'd had to retrieve from the DMV, as Kevin had no adult criminal record.

The bartender glanced at it and then looked closer. "Sure, the picture sucks but that's KD. Kevin something. He's in here all the time."

"Do you know if he was here on Thursday night?"

"Sure, Thursday is Drag Night and KD is always here for that." The bartender had nodded toward a poster on the wall behind him.

"Drag Night?"

"You know, a drag show. Lots of guys in dresses, Judy Garland imitations," Bobby interjected.

He turned away from Rocky's searching gaze. "I've just heard about them."

Turning back to the bar, Rocky confirmed, "So this KD is always here on Drag Night?"

"Sure, he helps Sweetpea with costumes and stuff." The bartender tapped the picture on the poster of a young blonde with a slash of scarlet lipstick. Her back was turned and she looked invitingly over her shoulder at the camera. The blade of glittering fabric she wore was cut down to the waist and up the leg to her hip. Rocky kind of envied the well-shaped booty that was all but exposed in the shot.

"That is a guy? A drag queen?"

"Yeah, she's something, isn't she?" The three of them gazed at the photo for several seconds. "And she's got pipes."

Rocky at least was grateful that she knew that having pipes meant someone could sing and didn't have to ask about that.

"So Sweetpea and KD are friends?"

"Sure, I guess you'd call them friends. KD is kind of her manager-with-benefits."

Rocky didn't even want to know what kind of benefits they were talking about, but it did shine a whole new light on Kevin Durbin.

"So, you can confirm that KD was here last Thursday night."

"I told you he is always here on Drag Night."

"Can you tell me whether he was here, in the club, the entire evening from say, eight to eleven o'clock?"

"I think so. I was busy. It's one of our biggest nights. I suppose he could have left at some point and come back. You'd probably have to talk to Sweetpea. She'd know better than me."

"Do you know where I can find Sweetpea?"

"Right around the corner at the coffee shop. She's a barista there. She could be working today. Name's Jason."

Rocky thanked the barkeep and motioned for Bobby to follow her out the door. The wan SF sunlight seemed blinding after the dark club and it took a minute to adjust their vision.

"The coffee place is to the right on the next block off Castro Street." Bobby motioned in that direction.

"After you."

They spotted Sweetpea's alter ego in regular street clothes as soon as they entered the shop. Even without the makeup and glitz his face was striking. He was smiling broadly as he surreptitiously slid his cell phone from his pocket, glancing around to see if anyone noticed him checking. His smile faded quickly and his eyes were wide when he looked up and saw Rocky and Bobby at the door. He gave one glance at the rear entrance but seemed to think better of trying to make a quick exit.

"I can help you here." This smile was not nearly as broad as the one they'd seen before.

"Yes… Jason," Rocky had noted the name badge he wore on his polo shirt. "We'd like to talk to you about your performance last week at Specs."

"Um, I'm working right now and my manager doesn't know anything about the other gig." He glanced nervously over his shoulder at the middle-aged man behind the counter.

"Well, we can talk here, or you can come down to the station." Rocky flipped open her badge, but she did lower her voice. No point in getting the kid in trouble.

"I'm due for a break in a few minutes. Can I get you coffee or something while you wait?"

"Sure, two black coffees." A couple of new customers had lined up behind them so they stepped aside.

"Can I help you?" Jason asked them.

"Yes, I'd like a grande skinny vanilla latte with three pumps of syrup with almond milk and a grande half-caf Americano."

It sounded like a foreign language to Rocky but Jason quickly tapped the order into the register.

Rocky and Bobby took their coffees to one of the tall bistro tables near the window and waited for Jason to take his break. He seemed open to talking to them, but Rocky still sat facing the counter in case he decided to slide out the back.

In about ten minutes they saw him speak with the manager and come around the counter toward their table.

"I don't know what you are here for, my act is pretty tame. I'm supposed to be Celine Dion, for crying out loud." Jason did look confused.

"This isn't really about your act. It's about your friend KD. Is this him?" Bobby pulled the picture of Kevin from his pocket and Jason's face paled.

"Yes, that's KD. Did something happen to him, is he hurt?"

Rocky responded quickly as it looked like the young man was about to pass out. "He's fine as far as we know. We're just following up on where he was on Thursday evening last week."

"We were at Specs like we usually are. I remember because I was surprised to see him. He was supposed to be going to see his grandmother in the castle on the hill."

Bobby nodded.

"The castle on the hill?" Once again Rocky was confused about some reference everyone else seemed to understand.

"The Towers up on Pine Street," Bobby volunteered. "Where he was supposed to go with Grace."

At the mention of Grace, a cloud crossed Jason's face. "He was going to take his girlfriend to have dinner with his grandmother." The word *girlfriend* screamed for air quotes, but Jason resisted the action.

"We spoke with Mr. Durbin about his plans and he told us he had gone to Specs instead. Can you confirm what hours Mr. Durbin was at the club with you?"

"I usually go on about ten p.m. and it takes a good hour for me to get dressed and warmed up, so I guess he showed up about seven-thirty. We stay at the club until it closes at two, kind of working the crowd… schmoozing."

"Was Mr. Durbin with you at the club the entire time from seven-thirty until two a.m.?"

"Yes, well, not when I'm on stage. I'm up there about an hour with my act and the group number I do with Judy and Adele."

"Judy Garland and Adele, the singers," Bobby whispered.

Rocky glared at him; she wasn't a complete idiot. "Do you know if he was there during your act?"

"Not really. You can't really see the crowd with the lights and everything."

"Where did you go after the club closed?"

"I was going to go straight home because I had an early shift on Friday morning, but KD was wired and wanted to go back to his place, so we did."

"Do you have any idea why Mr. Durbin would have been wired?"

"Sometimes he just is. I think he was pissed off at the girlfriend because she cancelled on him." There were the implied air quotation marks again.

"Okay, Jason. Thanks for your time. Here are the phone numbers for me and for Detective Burns. Call if you think of anything else." Rocky slid her card across the table.

Jason looked at it like it might bite him but picked it up after a moment. "What's this all about? Is KD in trouble or something?" Rocky could almost see the moment Jason noted that the card said she was from Homicide. "This is about a murder? Who's dead?"

"Grace Callahan, KD's girlfriend, was murdered in her condo on Thursday night."

Jason's face paled, but he didn't say anything.

"Please give Detective Burns your telephone number and we will let you know when you can come in and sign a statement." Rocky took the cold coffee to the trash bin and dumped it out while Bobby got the phone information from Jason.

Bobby glanced back as they left the shop. "How long do you think it will take before he texts or calls KD?"

"I don't know, but I think Mr. Durbin won't be happy with the flimsy alibi he gave him. An hour on stage would have been plenty of time for someone to get from Specs to Alamo Square and back."

CHAPTER THIRTY-SEVEN

Thursday, July 8

The more Kestrel thought about Kevin Durbin and his tenuous relationship with his grandmother, Lilah, and her money, the more she wondered if Kevin had something to do with Grace's death.

It took only a few minutes for her to fire up the laptop and find out where he lived. It was still early in the day and she imagined that he was the type to sleep late. Getting dressed, she took special care to make herself invisible. She hesitated over pulling the VW out of the garage but realized that she might need to follow Kevin and she had no idea if he foolishly tried to maintain a car in the Marina District or utilized public transit like most San Franciscans did. She needed to be able to follow him, whatever mode of transportation he used, so she threw her purse and laptop bag into the car and wound her way through the city. She was lucky and found a parking spot on his block. It was going to be difficult to monitor the front door of his building from the position she was in, so she crossed the street and stationed herself in the front window of a little café. She opened the laptop and pulled out her phone. She needed to follow up on some of her blog stories and wanted to polish the latest post. She'd been waiting for more information from a couple of contacts and this would be a good time to get it.

It had been a couple of hours since she'd arrived and she realized she would need to move the car or feed the meter soon. She was finishing up the last bits on the blog post when she saw Kevin come out the front door of his building. She snapped the computer shut and slipped it into her bag, threw a ten-dollar bill on the table, and went out to the street. Kevin had stopped to open the trunk of a low-slung car and lifted the case he was carrying into the back of it. Kestrel headed for her own car. The timing was perfect, as she'd been able to swing out of the parking spot and pull into traffic just a couple of cars behind Kevin as he drove away. She followed him to a dry cleaner where he picked up a long garment bag, and then through several blocks of the Castro District as he looked for a parking place. When he had finally maneuvered the car into a mostly legal street spot she zipped across Castro and parked in the lot of a grocery store. Locking the car, she dashed back just as he turned the corner. She hurried to catch up and almost ran into him as he stopped to enter a coffee shop. She turned her head away from him and hurried past as he entered. Once she was sure he hadn't seen her she turned back and stationed herself outside the coffee shop with a clear view of the interior.

The young barista at the counter seemed to know him and they chatted for a couple of minutes before he took his coffee and found a stool at one of the tall tables. He pulled his phone from his pocket and gave it his full concentration. Kestrel leaned against the outside wall and watched him play Candy Crush or whatever for the next half hour. At six p.m. the barista removed his apron and came out from behind the counter. Kestrel was not shocked but was surprised to see the young man slide his arm around Kevin's shoulder and lean in to give him a much more than friendly kiss. Kevin slipped his own arm around the barista's waist and whispered something in his ear. He put his phone back in his pocket and the two left the café arm in arm. They walked back to Kevin's car and unloaded the case and garment bag from the trunk, walked about a half a block, talking and laughing, and entered what looked like a church except for the neon signs and gaudy posters.

The guard at the door let them in, but a few minutes later, when Kestrel tried to follow, the man stopped her.

"We're not open until eight o'clock."

"Oh, I thought I saw some people just enter."

"That's the talent, we don't open until eight."

"I'll come back then. Thanks."

CHAPTER THIRTY-EIGHT

Thursday, July 8

When Kestrel got back to her duplex, a sticky-note had been stuck on her door, "You got a package, I left it on your table."

The one disadvantage to the small mailboxes and door-to-door delivery she still got was that packages of almost any size did not fit in the box. So, they would get left on the step within view of the street and in the line of blustery rain. There was a good chance anything left there would either disappear or be too soggy to identify by the time she got home. She and Sam had early-on made a pact to put each other's packages inside. Having someone else keep your house key could be invaluable if you could trust them, and there was probably nobody she knew that was more trustworthy than Sam.

She'd stopped at Trader Joe's on the way home and wrangled her bags through the door, dumping them on the counter before closing the door behind her. She loved living close to a TJs but she almost always bought more than she'd intended and gravely regretted the impulse purchases by the time she had lugged the bags the two blocks to her kitchen. She'd bought a shopping cart on Amazon, but unfortunately never had it with her when she actually needed it. Besides, it would have made her feel like an upscale bag lady if she'd used it (upscale because she'd purchased it rather than absconded with it from some neighborhood market).

Sam had rescued her regular mail along with the package and she filled the electric kettle and got it started before she sat down at the table to check it out. Junk, junk, ad, flyer, catalogue...crap! Nobody sent anything interesting by snail mail anymore. She didn't recall ordering anything from Amazon and didn't recognize the return address on the padded envelope. Ripping it open she removed a piece of notepaper and a bulging leather-covered notebook wrapped with an elastic band.

> Kestrel,
>
> You don't know me. I was a close friend of Grace Callahan and she told me about you. I helped her parents clean out her condo on the weekend and this was under her mattress. You can see that she had written your name and address on one of the last pages. I thought you might want to have something of hers, so I am sending it to you.

The note was just signed "Doug" and had a phone number written under the signature.

Kestrel picked up the book. It was a journal of sorts, or a sketchpad, that was inserted into a tooled leather cover that could be used again. The cover was embossed "Grace Callahan" in gold and the first page of the pad inside had been dated January 1.

Kestrel wanted both to devour the notations and pictures and to hide the book under her bed to gather dust until some future time when she felt she could read it.

Instead of either choice she turned off the kettle, poured herself a cup of tea, and began to put away the groceries: several salads that would go bad in the back of the vegetable crisper before she got around to eating them, various unusual frozen food items that had caught her eye. Those would fare better because of their longer shelf life. There were a couple of bottles of Two Buck Chuck, cheap but serviceable, and a tub of dark chocolate peanut butter cups, for emergencies.

She threw out the junk mail, checked her phone messages, posted some titillating comments on both Instagram and Twitter, poured out her now-tepid tea and refilled the cup with wine.

Finally, she sat down at the table, took a couple of good swallows of the wine, and began leafing through the book. There were not a lot of soul-searching confidences written here. Grace seemed to draw or write something most days; sketches depicting scenes from her day, sometimes a sentence or two, with photographs and mementos stuck into the pages, stubs from movie tickets, a cartoon torn from *The New Yorker*, an ad for something she admired, or a recipe torn from a magazine. Kestrel could imagine her sitting in the waiting room at the dentist's office ripping the page from an old issue of *Family Circle*. She would have looked around stealthily and coughed to cover the sound of the paper tearing.

On the second mug of wine Kestrel turned to the final entries in the book… The last page, done on the day Grace had died, showed a sketch of a building Kestrel recognized immediately, The Towers. There were hearts drawn at the four corners of the page and the words, "I feel so sorry for Lilah…" written at the bottom of the drawing.

Turning back to an earlier page, Kestrel found the receipts for their visit to the Academy of Sciences and a drawing of sunflowers and children with writing curling between the flowers.

On the date Grace had met with her brother there was a sketch of a dark-haired man and a woman with a disappointed face, probably Grace herself. A few days before that, there was a coaster from Specs and a drawing of Grace and three men at a table. Beneath the drawing she'd written, "Doug and his dads." In the background there was a man and a woman with the word "Kevin" with a question mark.

Kestrel looked at the drawing for a few minutes and finished her wine before she pulled out her phone and punched in the number written beneath Doug's name on the note.

The call lasted into the night. Doug had a lot to say about Grace, and about Kevin. It was obvious that Kestrel was not the only one swigging wine while they talked. "There's a note about you and your dads being at Specs. Did anything unusual happen that night?"

"Not really, just that Grace was kind of quiet when we left. I asked her if anything was wrong but she laughed it off. Said she thought she'd seen someone she knew."

Kestrel had a chance to ask a few other questions before the call devolved into a mutual sniffle-fest.

At some point she had taken the phone with her into her bedroom, and since she woke up still dressed on top of the bedspread with the phone still in her hand, she thought it likely she had fallen asleep in the middle of the call.

CHAPTER THIRTY-NINE

Saturday, July 10

On Saturday morning Kestrel hoped her car would not start as she wasn't sure she wanted to go on this particular journey. But little workhorse that it was, the VW fired right up after only a cough and a sputter.

Kestrel had not ventured down the San Francisco Peninsula on Highway 280 for several years, not since her grandmother had died and the house in Palo Alto had been sold. During her childhood her grandmother's home had been both a penance and a sanctuary. Her stays there were usually the result of some adventure her mother had undertaken and these could take a few weeks or a winter, and once, when she was in high school, an entire year. Her grandmother had accepted her presence as she did all the annoying vicissitudes of life. She was not a warm woman, but she was sweet in her artsy, slightly dim way. Kestrel was welcome there, as a traveling wayfarer. She was not mistreated as much as ignored. One summer she'd ventured out from her room to discover that Grandma Dolores had apparently forgotten she was there and gone off for a few days to paint. Kestrel was self-sufficient and relished a few days pretending to be a grown-up all on her own. When Dolores returned she was surprised to find Kestrel there, but, since everything was fine, went on about her life.

The memorial service for Grace at Stanford University chapel was set for ten a.m. so Kestrel decided to begin her drive south early to beat the impossible Bay Area traffic, heavy even on a weekend. The fog still blanketed San Francisco, and it was pleasant to drive down "the world's most beautiful freeway" and see the wisps of cloud diminish and the sun break through the veil. That dubious title became popular in the nineteen-sixties when the roadway was opened, although the signs proclaiming it as such were knocked down years ago. Still, it did beat the heck out of driving down its ugly stepsister, Highway 101, maybe the ugliest freeway in the world.

Once out of San Francisco Kestrel could focus less on the driving and more on the purpose of the drive. She had decided, after much gnashing of teeth, to attend the service. She would not know a single person there, really didn't even know Grace, but felt compelled to pay this one tiny bit of acknowledgment to their connection. She was wearing her usual disguise of black slacks and a white shirt, but she'd added a black blazer and flats. She wasn't sure if she was dressing up or dressing down, she just knew she wanted to be there today to hear what people had to say about the sister she would never really know.

She rolled onto the campus and parked in the circle of visitor parking in front of Stanford Memorial Church. She sat in her car drinking her venti latte and nibbling her scone until five minutes before ten, then locked the car, walked across the plaza and entered the historic building. The chapel was large, and small individual events were allocated to the lesser vestibules. She followed the signs for the Grace Callahan service and slipped into the last pew just as the music began.

The chapel was dim and quiet and she looked over the program she had picked up on the way in. She heard people speak about Grace. She had been serious, sometimes funny (although from the varied recollections Kestrel couldn't tell if they meant funny strange or funny ha-ha). She was a good student and she was a loving daughter and granddaughter. The program had pictures of her life growing up, playing soccer, in her Castilleja uniform, her prom, and graduation pictures. Kestrel wasn't sure what connection she had hoped to gain here, but all of this was foreign to her and was about a stranger. She had intended to slip out the door before the service ended so there would be no need to explain her presence but had been arrested by the first words of the final prayer, and although she didn't know who she prayed to, or why, she found herself agreeing that "our lovely Grace should be in heaven" or in whatever place she had gone. As she had stood with her eyes closed and her head bowed, she barely perceived the quiet but rapid footsteps that passed her and proceeded out into the open foyer. She kept her eyes closed for several seconds after the final amen and then picked up her bag and, head down, bolted for the exit.

Not watching where she was going, she walked directly into a woman standing in the entry. Instinctively she reached out to steady the woman and gazed into her eyes. The eyes widened and the woman gasped. "Grace? Gracie?"

"No, no, I'm just a friend. Sorry, so sorry." And then Kestrel almost ran for the parking lot, leaving the woman and her male companion staring after her.

Before she could reach the safety of her car the man caught up with her. "Wait, please wait..." he huffed. She could tell that he was not used to running and he looked like he might collapse as he leaned forward with his hands on his knees trying to catch his breath.

Jesus, this was not going as planned. She hadn't meant to even speak to anyone, much less have anyone see her resemblance to Grace.

She opened her car door, calculating that she could move the VW around him and be gone before he said any more.

"Please don't." He reached his arm toward her and the look on his face halted her flight. "You must be the sister Grace told us about. We were just so shocked. You look so much like her."

"I know, I'm sorry. I didn't mean to upset anything. I just felt if I came today I might know her better. That sounds dumb. I'm just so sorry."

"No, no, don't be sorry. Don't leave yet. I am, was, Grace's dad. Please come back and meet her mother."

"I can't, I have to work today." Kestrel slid into the car seat.

"Okay, okay, I can see this isn't a good time. But, please, this has been such a terrible time for us. There will be too many people today, too much to explain. Please say you will come back and see just us. Talk to us." He reached into his jacket pocket and pulled out a card. "Here, take my card, call me when you have a day off. Come see Grace's home, come help us to understand."

Reluctantly, Kestrel took the card from his hand. "I will come and see you, but not until I have something I can tell you."

He seemed to understand and said nothing more as she closed the door and fired up the car. The drive back to SF was even more confusing than the drive down had been.

CHAPTER FORTY

Monday, July 12

Gari had managed to keep the cooperative smile on his face even as his hand shook closing the door behind Detectives Stafford and Brown. He stood stone still with his hand still on the doorknob until Mary's voice behind him caused him to turn in fury.

"This is all your damned fault, you insisted on getting my DNA tested for the kids' school projects."

Mary gaped at him, her mouth closing and opening like a goldfish. She'd been ready to light into him demanding answers about why the police were coming to the house: what would the neighbors say, what had he done now, why hadn't he told her what was going on? All those questions had popped into her head as she had sat in her lovely living room, smiling benignly, and hearing her husband deny and then admit to talking to George, of all people, about a sister, or maybe sisters. She was still confused on that part.

When the police had first arrived, Gari had tried to get Mary to leave the interview to him, but there was no way she wasn't sticking around to hear what was going on. He'd welcomed them, a smile frozen on his face except when replaced with a look of earnest concern.

"Detective, good to see you. Have you found out any new information about that poor girl?"

"Actually, we do have a few more insights into the murder and some additional questions for you."

"I told you I never met with that girl. Even her sister said it wasn't me she talked about, right?"

"Well, yes, but Ms. Jonas also managed to send us a picture of you meeting with a friend of yours, one of your attorneys, we believe." Rocky held up her phone with the picture of Gari meeting with George at Tommy's Joynt.

"Yes, he's my brother-in-law. We were just having a beer. We get together all the time."

"Of course, that makes perfect sense. Thank you for clarifying. Let me get some clarification from you on an unrelated matter."

"Sure, anything I can do to help."

Rocky opened the folder she carried. "We have records here that indicate that you have withdrawn over one hundred thousand dollars in cash from your various accounts over the past couple of weeks." Rocky checked her notes again. "All of it since you received the first email from Grace Callahan."

Gari considered for a moment, avoiding Mary's intense gaze, before deciding to go on the offensive. "Those are my private financial dealings! You have no right to be snooping around in my business."

"On the contrary, Mr. Graham. In a murder investigation we have very broad authority to look for evidence. The appropriate documents were received for this inquiry. I'm surprised your banks didn't notify you."

Mary said nothing but realized a bit too late that she probably should have mentioned the voicemail messages from a couple of banks last week. She'd forgotten all about them.

Rocky closed the file folder. "Do you want to tell us why you were in such a hurry to acquire quite a lot of cash?"

"Mary, could you get us some coffee, please?" Gari barked out, but Mary did not move from her perch on the edge of the love seat.

Friendship was important, but it took Gari about ten seconds to decide it was necessary to give George up to the police. On consideration he knew that George would throw him under the bus in a heartbeat to save his own skin and this was Gari's chance to make the first move.

"All right. You must understand that I was shocked when I received an email from a woman, a stranger to me, saying that she thought we were related. I didn't want to upset my family about it until I could find out if it was true, so I talked to my brother-in-law, George Musgrove. He's a lawyer, so I thought he might know what to do."

"I see, did Mr. Musgrove have any ideas?"

"Yes, well actually, I think it was my idea after we talked. I thought he might answer the email and see what the woman was like, what she wanted from us. I mean, it could have been a hoax. There's been a lot of press coverage about my father's trust and the family's suit to overturn it. She could have just been someone trying to get money out of us."

Mary nodded in the background.

"Did Mr. Musgrove, George, contact Ms. Callahan?"

"Yes, he contacted her and I think he met with her. I didn't know until later that he told her he was her brother and gave her a fake name."

"So, Mr. Musgrove told you that he met with Ms. Callahan and then what?"

"He said she wanted money. That it might not be a hoax but she was willing to take some money and move to Mexico or somewhere. It only had to be until the court case was settled and the inheritance taken care of."

"It seems you forgot to mention discussing this with George Musgrove when we interviewed you at the station."

"I just wanted to talk to George first, see what was going on." Gari was beginning to feel defensive.

"Did you give the money to Ms. Callahan?"

"No, I told you I never met her. I gave it to George to pass along to her. I only had sixty thousand at first, but I gave him the rest later."

"Did Mr. Musgrove tell you he gave the money to Ms. Callahan?"

Gari considered the question for a moment. "Not exactly, but he did suggest that maybe somebody she knew killed her for the money."

"So, you talked to Mr. Musgrove about this after the murder?"

"Well, yes, after I talked to you at the police station, I got in touch with George to see what he had to say."

"And what did he have to say?"

"That she must have been killed for the money. Did the police find the money?"

"No large sums of money were found at the murder scene."

"Well, there you are. Someone must have taken it."

"Are you sure that Mr. Musgrove gave the money to Ms. Callahan?"

"Of course, what else would he do with it?" Gari's voice did not sound quite as confident as before.

"I guess we'll have to talk to him about that. Do you know where we might find Mr. Musgrove today?"

"He's probably at his office, or they will know where he is."

Rocky stood up and Bobby followed her lead. She turned to Mary and asked just one question. "Mrs. Graham, were you aware of any of these activities?"

Mary just shook her head. When Gari escorted the detectives to the door she followed him, stopping at the entrance to the living room.

CHAPTER FORTY-ONE

Monday, July 12

The reverberations from the front door slamming were still echoing through the house when Mary grabbed up her phone and called Amélie, who was far down on the favorites list, right after Gari's cell, Gari's office, her mother, her sister Bridget, the kids' school, her hairdresser, and the housekeeper.

The discussion with Gari had not gone well before he stormed out of the house. When he left, she didn't have a lot more information than she'd had when the police left. In his usual fashion he had immediately made whatever had gone on in his life someone else's fault. In this case, her fault for insisting on a DNA sample from him and George's fault for mucking everything up.

The phone rang unanswered until the message carefully recorded in Amélie's sometimes prissy voice chimed in.

The beep had hardly sounded before she spoke. "I know you are screening, Amélie. Pick up the damned phone!" She was ready to hang up when Amélie finally picked up the receiver.

"What do you want, Mary, I was still sleeping." The voice did not sound welcoming.

"This is going to wake you up in a lot of ways, kiddo. Did you know that Gari has another sister and the police are asking about George?"

"No, I don't know any such thing, and why would George be involved?"

"Well, apparently Gari asked George to buy her off and now she's been murdered."

The silence on the other end of the phone was almost palpable for several seconds. "I don't understand what you're talking about, Mary. What is going on?"

Finally assured of Amélie's complete attention Mary launched into her story.

"Two police detectives, Homicide detectives, came to the house this morning. Gari knew them and tried to get me to leave the room, but I wasn't about to go anywhere. They had talked to him before but he never mentioned anything to me."

"Why did they want to talk to him again?"

"It seems there was a little detail he'd left out about sending George to meet this woman and giving him a shit-load of money to buy her off."

The mention of money captured Amélie's attention even more than before. Murder wasn't a trigger for her, but money definitely was. "How much money?"

Mary considered for a moment whether it was odd that Amélie hadn't bothered to ask about the murdered woman but was intent on the money. Then, remembering who she was talking to, she went on. "One. Hundred. Thousand. Dollars… in cash."

Amélie gasped audibly. A hundred thousand dollars was not that much in the big picture of their world, where millions were in play at any moment. Still, it was a chunk of change to be throwing around. "Who was this woman? How did she contact Gari?"

Mary hesitated for a moment before responding. "Well, you know how we wanted to get DNA information for the kids' school project?"

"Yeah, I remember. George absolutely refused. Said he didn't want to know any more about either family than he already did."

"Gari wasn't thrilled but I don't think he cared that much. My family had already done it before so we decided he was the person who would do it. I never gave it another thought. I guess he got the information but didn't really look at it. I'd forgotten all about it."

"If he didn't look at it, how did he know about the sister?"

"She contacted him, sent him an email through the DNA company. When he got the email he kind of freaked out. He mentioned it to George because he thought it might be a scam; you know, with the court case about the trust being in the paper, and all."

"The trust! Could this new person impact that? Could she get part of the estate?"

"That's what Gari asked George."

"George is a tax attorney." The disdain in Amélie's voice was clear.

"Anyway, Gari suggested that George respond to the girl's email and check out her story and George said he would."

"Then what happened?" Amélie had started to piece some of the events of the past couple of weeks together and one of the first pieces was the private detective's report she had received. She climbed out of bed and went to her office where the skimpy report she'd received along with Lester Stuyvesant's invoice, and ridiculous expense report, rested in a folder labeled Household Expenses. She'd known that nobody entering her office would ever bother opening that folder.

"George said he'd met with her. He told Gari that she wanted money to go away, but it seemed like she really was his dad's daughter."

It finally had occurred to Amélie that this woman was her sister, as well. "I can't believe she just wanted money from us!" Her indignation would have been funny if Mary wasn't so upset.

"It doesn't matter what she wanted, Amélie, she's dead, and somebody killed her. They think Gari had something to do with it, and George."

"Do you know what her name is, was?"

"Calhoun, or something like that. She lived over near Alamo Square."

Amélie abruptly sat down at the desk and pulled the folder toward her. "I have to go, Mary, I'll call you later."

By the time Mary could respond she heard the dial tone. "Shit!"

Amélie flipped the file folder open and then pulled her laptop over. It didn't take long to find the newspaper report of a recent homicide on Fulton Street. Grace Callahan at 988 Fulton. The address where George had been seen dropping a woman off jumped off the page.

Amélie picked up the phone and dialed her most-used number. "Dixon, it's me."

CHAPTER FORTY-TWO

Monday, July 12

Claiming an off-site meeting, George was taking his time returning to the office. He'd stopped for a haircut at the swanky shop on the ground floor of his building, bought a paper and a latte at the coffee shop, and was about to head into the elevator when his cell phone rang.

Damn, that admin couldn't leave a guy alone for a minute. He'd already told her he was in a meeting. Sighing mightily, he took the call. "What is it, Connie? I'm almost there."

"Mr. Musgrove, there were two police officers here looking for you." She paused for a moment, then added breathlessly, "Two Homicide detectives."

George nearly dropped the latte and the phone. "I am sure it is nothing. I'm a few blocks away and have a couple of errands to run, so I'll be in a little later. When were the officers there?"

"They just left, they just got on the elevator. I called you right away."

"Thank you, that was the right thing to do. I'm sure it's nothing to be concerned about. If they come back just tell them you expect me in a little later today."

George barely had time to duck behind a pillar before the elevator door opened and out strode a Black woman and a tall man, both of whom looked very official. "Shit, shit, shit."

Once George was sure that the police had gone, he ducked down the stairwell to the parking garage. He wondered if they might have someone watching his car but had to take the chance. They had no reason to think he was in the building so they probably wouldn't think of it.

Once he had circled a few blocks in the car he felt it was safe to head home. Driving past his house he noted an unfamiliar car parked in the driveway first, and then the two detectives he'd seen at the office standing at the top of the steps talking to Amélie. He kept driving right on past the house and hoped his wife had not spotted his car. In the rearview mirror he saw them go into the house and the door close behind them.

***

It was Gari's turn to not take George's frantic calls. After he'd stormed out of the house leaving Mary behind in the entryway he'd driven around the city and ended up sitting in the back parking lot of the PU Club. He didn't know why he'd gone there. It just seemed like a refuge in some way. A private place that not even George could get into uninvited.

When the calls from George started coming he'd turned his phone off completely. He was still stung by his friend's possible betrayal, but even more appalled by how quickly he had given his old buddy up to the police. He could believe that George would have killed someone before he would believe his friend would turn on him just for money. It had only occurred to him when he was talking to the police that he didn't know where that money had gone. He'd sounded like a fool, and now he began to feel like one, as well.

***

Amélie had been expecting the police. Dixon had let her know that they had gone to the law office first but that George was not in yet. The obvious next stop was their home.

She was so lucky to have Dixon right now. He was levelheaded and a little older. He loved her and would protect her. He'd told her exactly what to do. If she'd been married to Dixon no police would ever have come to disturb her peace.

"Just tell them the truth, Amélie. You have nothing to hide."

"I know, but can't you come over here and be with me?"

He was right that it would look unnecessarily suspicious if she'd already pulled in her attorney. If she needed him, she could call and ask him to come over.

When they rang the bell, she was standing right by the door, but waited for a bit before opening it, taking a couple of deep breaths to steady her nerves. She'd acted appropriately surprised to find Homicide police on her doorstep. "Please come in, officers. What can I do for you?"

"Thank you, Mrs. Musgrove. We were wondering if your husband is at home this morning."

"Why no, he left for his office at the usual time today." Nothing but the truth. "Do you need the address?"

"No, ma'am. We've already been to his office and he wasn't there. We thought he might be here."

"Oh, dear, that's strange." Don't let them suspect you already heard that from Dixon.

"Well, while we are here, we have a couple of questions for you. Do you have a few minutes to speak with us?"

"Certainly, please come into the living room. Would you like some coffee?" Amélie smiled and gestured toward the other room. She felt oddly like she was in a play.

They asked a lot of questions about the night they had gone to the opera. When did they leave, where did they eat, who was with them? She mentioned that George had not sat with them but met them during intermission.

"What time was intermission, Mrs. Musgrove?"

"I don't know exactly, but the production started at eight and it was probably nine-thirty or so. They usually combine Acts One and Two and then Three and Four for *Il Trovatore*."

"So, you didn't see your husband between eight and nine-thirty that evening."

"No, as I said, he gave up his seat for my friend that night and got a seat someplace else."

"Has your husband ever mentioned a woman named Grace Callahan to you?"

"No, he's never mentioned her to me, but I believe he knows her."

"Do you know how he knows her?"

This was Amélie's favorite part of the interview. She hemmed and hawed a bit, looked sheepish, and then admitted to having George followed by a private detective.

"And the private detective's report mentioned Grace Callahan?"

"Yes, but it didn't say anything bad, just that George had dinner with her a couple of weeks ago and then dropped her at her apartment. I feel silly really, that I was suspicious that George was seeing someone else. But it turned out to be nothing."

"Do you have a copy of the report?"

"I'm sure I can find it, if you need it." Of course, she knew exactly where it was as she had already read it to Dixon and, on his advice, made a photocopy of it for the police. It took just a couple of minutes for her to go to her office to retrieve it, but she made a point of spending a little time tidying her desk before she returned, so they would believe that she'd had to actually look for it.

Once the police had left it occurred to Amélie that George might come home. That she might have to tell him about the discussion. Through the kitchen window she could see Rocky and Bobby sitting in the car in the driveway making their notes when Amélie once more made a call to Dixon. He'd know what she should do.

CHAPTER FORTY-THREE

Tuesday, July 13 – Wednesday, July 14

Amélie needn't have fretted about explaining things to George because he didn't come home on Monday night or on Tuesday.

He'd spent most of his time debating with himself how much the police might know and trying to come up with a good story. On one hand he thought he might have a good shot at explaining everything away until he could find out how deep his troubles ran. But he feared more that they would just toss him in jail if he showed up.

He'd hung out at a couple of bars and coffee shops messing around on his laptop using their free Wi-Fi, drinking endless cups of coffee and more beer than he was used to. Neither the caffeine nor the alcohol was a benefit to clear thinking.

Checking out his resources on Monday night, he'd come up with a couple of hundred dollars in cash and had stopped quickly at an ATM and withdrawn what he could but was afraid to use his credit cards at a hotel. He'd driven down the Peninsula and found a hotel not far from the airport that didn't ask a lot of questions and took cash. He'd have jumped on a plane or filled the car with gas and driven out of state if he'd had any idea where to go. For the first time he realized that Amélie and her family were his only safe haven. He didn't even have any friends outside that circle.

On Tuesday night he'd spotted a police car in the parking lot of the hotel when he returned and was afraid to stay there another night. He'd slept in his car in the airport parking lot.

By Wednesday morning he'd decided that he needed to get into his office and to his hidden cache of stuff. His passport was there, his cash, a couple of credit cards, pretty much everything he owned, and he couldn't do anything without that. Maybe he could buy himself some time to hire an attorney and see what kind of trouble he was in. Or maybe he could take what he had and get out of the country. People disappeared all the time, although he couldn't really envision himself living in a hut on some beach trying to get by on fish and beer.

He decided that it would be best to go into the office after everyone left on Wednesday. He'd get in, grab his stuff, and get out. Then he'd decide what to do next.

***

The SFPD hadn't spent a lot of time looking for George Musgrove. They figured he'd turn up eventually, and by then they'd have their case against him all set to go.

The fingerprints from the light bulb at Mrs. Woodstock's apartment had been a match for the ones from George's office. They'd been able to get a statement from Lester Stuyvesant about his report. The search warrant for his home had come up a bust, but the one for his office had been much more interesting.

No credit card activity and only one ATM withdrawal had come up, so they figured he'd have to come looking for the stash of cash locked in his desk before long.

A stakeout of the office on Tuesday had yielded nothing, but they weren't ready to give up yet.

Wednesday night a small group of people sat up late in the law office. The admins and even the associate attorneys, who worked horrendous hours, had gone home. They all sat in Dixon Donahue's office with the lights turned off, though quite a bit of light came in from the city lights beyond the windows.

Detectives Raquel Stafford and Bobby Burns were there, and Amélie Musgrove and her very close friend—and George's boss—Dixon Donahue. Kestrel had asked to be there, although it wasn't strictly kosher, and there were a couple of armed police officers. There was a little hushed talking, and all of them were about ready to call it a day when they heard the distinctive click of the outer office door being unlocked.

They couldn't hear footfalls on the plush office carpet, but then they heard the click of the lock to George's office.

George had been loitering in the hallway for some time, assuring himself that everyone had left the building. The inner waiting room was completely dark when he let himself in, all of the windows being allocated to the partners' offices. He'd felt his way cautiously across the room and located his own office door, grateful for the mini flashlight on his key ring. It was difficult to fit the key into the lock in the darkness, but when the door swung open, he breathed a sigh of relief. He didn't dare turn on the overhead lights but felt his way to his desk and clicked on the lamp.

He unlocked the bottom drawer of the desk and felt a swell of excitement that all of his belongings seemed to be there.

"Hello, George." A woman stood in the door of the office, the light from the lamp casting shadows over her face.

He jumped and slammed the drawer shut. "You can't be here. You're not real."

"I'm as real as you are."

"No… you're dead, I saw you."

"Not me, George, my sister Grace. Are you going to kill me too?" The woman stepped into the office and behind her came his wife, and his boss, and the police.

"I didn't kill her. I didn't. She was already dead when I got there."

"Hey, Bobby, have you ever heard that one before?" Rocky stepped into the room.

"Sure, lots of times. If she was already dead, how did she let you into the apartment George?"

"She didn't let me in, it was already open. She was already dead."

Rocky cocked her head at him. It was surprising how sincere he sounded. "If you didn't kill her, why didn't you come give us a statement then?"

"I didn't think you'd believe me. I mean, I took her laptop and her phone, but nothing else. I didn't touch anything else."

"Why did you take her electronics?"

"So there'd be no connection to Gari and to me. I just dumped them with some guy over on Hayes Street. You can probably find him. He hangs out by that garbage can..." He stopped there. It even sounded stupid to him.

"Okay, makes sense, right, Bobby? But why did you stake out her condo from across the street?"

Trapped now, George admitted, "I thought about killing her, I thought I was going to, but she was already dead. It was like a miracle. I didn't have to do anything, just get out of there. She was already dead."

The conversation continued in this vein as they read George his rights, confiscated his loot, cuffed him, and led him out onto the elevator.

Kestrel and Bobby stood in front of the office building and watched as Detective Stafford climbed into the police cruiser with George. The flashing red-and-blue lights illuminated the street, and curious pedestrians ogled the scene. Dixon and Amélie had remained in the law offices. Kestrel imagined they were having a stiff drink right now, or maybe they had opened a bottle of champagne. After all, Gari was off the hook for Grace's murder, and Dixon and Amélie could live happily ever after. Their cozy relationship had been pretty obvious.

Officers from the Crime Scene van parked at the curb had begun pawing through George's drawer of treasures.

***

Kestrel was still shaken by witnessing George's frantic denials of guilt in Grace's murder. She guessed that all murderers denied their crimes with the same vehemence, but she hadn't expected to feel sorry for the little shit.

As the black-and-white drove off, Kestrel looked sideways at Bobby Burns. He looked tired, and much older than he had been a year before. This transfer to Homicide had been what he'd longed for, but maybe he wasn't cut out for it. She recalled the lazy Sunday mornings lying in the wan sunlight coming through the windows of her bedroom when he had talked about having the chance to solve real crimes and make a difference. She suspected that it hadn't been all he had thought it would be, but then, what really was? She had just scooped the biggest story of her investigative reporter career, but she didn't feel particularly celebratory.

In the big picture what difference did it all make? Grace was dead, George was a greedy little man driven over the edge by money, and, oddly enough, Kestrel had just begun to think about talking to Sam about what her connection with the filthy-rich Graham family might mean. Suddenly envisioning the greed in her mother's eyes should she begin to contemplate the possibilities made her shake off the notion.

"So, are you off duty, or what?"

"Yep, until tomorrow when all hell breaks loose with the press. Shouldn't you be rushing home to write this up for your blog?"

"I don't think I'm quite ready for that. I don't have to beat the papers, you know. I just have to have information they don't have."

"I guess."

"Do you want to go get a drink or something?"

"Maybe tomorrow. It's late and we are both beat. Let me drive you home."

"Okay," was all she could think of to say.

CHAPTER FORTY-FOUR

Thursday, July 15

Bobby stood in the hallway outside the interrogation room and yawned mightily. The sludgy cup of lukewarm coffee he held was the third of the morning and wasn't helping him much. He'd slept little and poorly after George's arrest.

"Well, you're here early, Detective Burns." Rocky Stafford's voice behind him made him jump and some of the coffee slopped onto the already dingy floor.

"Geez, don't sneak up on a guy like that. I might shoot you."

Rocky just rolled her eyes at him. She held a file folder in one hand and her cell phone in the other. "Are you ready?"

"Not really. What is your take on this guy?"

"Well, we know he was at the apartment, that he took the laptop and phone, that he made elaborate plans for that night, that he scoped out the place ahead of time, and that he met with the victim and lied to her about who he was. What else is there to know?"

"Shit, I don't know, I just don't think he's our guy."

"Yeah, I know, neither do I, but we have to go with the facts and they're pretty grim."

"I hate it when I feel sorry for the suspects. I feel like I'm bulldozing them."

"All we can do is talk to him and get his side of the story, so are you ready to do that?"

"I guess so." Bobby opened the door and Rocky walked past him into the room.

George was in a whispered conversation with his attorney, one Martin D'onofrio, the leading defense attorney in San Francisco. No public defender for a member of the Graham family.

The past few hours and a high-powered lawyer had revived some of his bravado and he looked more confident than he had in his mug shot.

"I am Detective Raquel Stafford and this is my partner, Detective Robert Burns. We will be conducting this interview with Mr. Musgrove and taping will begin now."

The attorney stood and extended his hand first to Rocky and then to Bobby. "I am Mr. Musgrove's attorney, Martin Denofrio. Nice to meet you both." He glanced and nodded toward George, who grudgingly stood.

When they were all seated Rocky opened the folder she'd been carrying and spoke. "Mr. Musgrove has had his *Miranda* rights previously explained to him. Do you have any questions?"

"No, but…" George began until Denofrio placed a hand gently on his arm.

"My client understands his rights, and I would like to state up front that we are sure that a review of the circumstances will clear up any suspicions regarding his involvement with Miss Callahan's unfortunate death."

"Good, then we can get started." Rocky looked down at the papers before her.

"Mr. Musgrove, do you know or have you ever met this woman, Grace Callahan?" She slid a picture of Grace across the table in front of George.

George barely glanced at the smiling photo. "Yes, I've met her once."

"Where did you meet Miss Callahan?"

"We met for dinner at a little place at the upper end of Hayes Valley."

"Do you recall the date you met?"

"Not exactly, it was a few weeks ago."

"Could you produce a credit card receipt or other proof of the date?"

"No, I paid cash for the meal."

"Do you usually pay cash for your meals in restaurants?"

Denofrio interrupted, "How my client usually pays for his meals is not pertinent here."

"All right. Then, can you tell me why you dined with Miss Callahan? Was it a date, or an interview?"

"No, I had arranged to meet with her to discuss her relationship to our family."

"And what was her relationship to your family?"

"Gari, that is Garrett Graham, had received an email from her saying that she was his half-sister."

"So, you decided to check it out."

"No, Gari asked me to check out whether it was legit, as his attorney."

"So, you contacted Miss Callahan as an attorney for the family and arranged to meet her for dinner?"

"Sort of. I didn't contact her as an attorney. I contacted her as her brother."

"You represented yourself as Mr. Graham."

George hesitated and glanced at Denofrio who nodded for him to continue. "I said my name was George Gregory, her brother."

"You gave her a fake name?"

"Yes, I didn't want to involve the Graham name, it's very well known in San Francisco."

"So, you told her you were her brother and gave her a fake name."

If D'onofrio was surprised he didn't show it. "Can we move forward with what occurred at this meeting?"

George began again. "We had dinner and it seemed like she might be related to the family. She didn't seem like she was trying to scam anyone or make a fuss. She seemed… nice, educated."

"What happened then?"

"She started talking about wanting to meet the family and I knew that was never going to happen."

"Why not?"

"Because the family is in the middle of a big court case trying to overturn the father's trust. The crazy old coot left most of his money to charities and we've been fighting it ever since he died. The last thing we need is a complication with stray kids coming out of the walls and claiming part of the fortune." George's voice had risen and D'onofrio again reached out and placed a calming hand on his arm.

"Look, I didn't have the authority to commit Gari and his sisters to meeting her, but I did have some money I could offer her to just sort of go away."

"Did you offer her money?"

"I mentioned giving her part of an inheritance, but nothing about going away."

"How did she take that?"

"Not very well, she seemed sort of angry, and maybe disappointed that I thought she wanted money."

"And how did you end the meeting?"

"I told her I hadn't told my, er, Gari's, sisters about her yet but could bring some family pictures for her to see. I offered to drive her home since it was getting dark and cold out."

"And did you drive her home?"

"Yes, I drove her to her place near Alamo Square and dropped her off, then I went home."

Rocky glanced down at her folder, but before she could continue, D'onofrio spoke. "I'd like to have a few minutes to consult with my client. Could we take a break?"

"Sure." Rocky and Bobby stood. "Can we get you anything? Water, coffee?"

"Nothing for me." D'onofrio's smile was stiff.

"Could I get a latte?" George said.

Bobby smiled. "Sure, I'll see what I can do."

He made a couple of phone calls and checked his email before pouring another cup of cop coffee and adding a big spoon of powdered creamer to it. "Latte, my ass."

He stood in the hallway with Rocky until D'onofrio opened the door to let them know they could resume the interview.

Rocky questioned George about the private detective's report, the surveillance of Grace's apartment as documented by his fingerprints on the light bulb, the stolen electronics, the pictures of Grace alone in her apartment found on George's cell phone, not to mention the hundred thousand dollars in cash stashed in his office desk, and all the other incriminating information they had gathered.

When they were done, Rocky and Bobby sat silently at their desks and pounded out their reports. At six o'clock Bobby shut down his computer and turned to Rocky's desk. "So, what do you think?"

Rocky, who had been staring out the window over the city responded, "I think we have a great case against the wrong guy."

"What are we going to do about it?"

"Well, I was just thinking the smartest thing I could do is close the case and finish my transfer to Vice. It's the DA's problem from now on."

"Really?"

"Yep, that's what I was thinking, but it's not what I'm feeling, dammit."

"Well, for tonight, I'm going to go see my friend Kestrel and try to forget this mess. Want to come along?"

"You mean as your wing-man?"

"Nope, you can be my date. Kestrel is my wing-man."

Rocky considered the offer for a moment, then laughed. "Nah, I just want to go home, have a glass of wine, a nice bubble bath, and finish binge-watching something on Netflix. I'm tired."

The two of them stepped into the elevator and parted on the steps of the station.

Bobby turned back to Rocky. "You know, once you transfer there's no reason we can't get to know each other better."

"I was thinking the same thing."

Bobby smiled. "Looking forward to it."

"Me, too."

CHAPTER FORTY-FIVE

Friday, July 15

A couple of hours later Bobby showed up at Kestrel's duplex bearing some flowers and a bottle of wine. "The wine is for you but the flowers are for Grace. I wish I'd had a chance to meet her."

"Thanks, Bobby, that's sweet. Tell you what, though, I'd really like to go somewhere. I've been here writing all day and trying to cope with everything. I need to get out."

Bobby looked at her speculatively. "You know, there is one thing I'd like to do. It's Thursday night. Drag Night at Specs. Have you ever been?"

"Not me. Do they have booze?"

"Oh, yeah."

"Well then, come with me." She linked arms with him and led him back to his car, parked just down the street.

The drag show at Specs had begun about twenty minutes before they got there. Kestrel was surprised that the place was so crowded, but this was rumored to be *the* drag show in San Francisco. She was skeptical, but once she'd settled at one of the bad tables by the restroom, she was fairly impressed by the style and talent onstage. It was nice to be able to just let go of all the stress of the past couple of weeks and enjoy the show.

The performers were charismatic and charming. For the most part they lip-synched from recordings, but a couple of them sang their own covers of the stars they were impersonating. The final number brought all of the performers together. By that point the audience was fully engaged, including Kestrel, and to a lesser extent, Bobby.

At the end of the show the performers filled the stage and the stage lights were brought up to full to assure everyone got their share of the glory. The final number, with a calypso beat, caused many of the audience members to form a conga line that snaked between and around the tables, with Kestrel joining in. When the number ended, she was across the room next to the stage when the line broke up. The singers came down off the stage into the audience and just in front of her, "Celine Dion" had been engulfed in the arms of a tall blond man. Their deep kiss lasted several moments and when the lip-lock finally ended it took Kestrel another few beats to recognize Kevin Durbin as one of the flushed participants. When he broke away and turned, he almost ran directly into her. He paled and came to an abrupt stop. "Grace?" he croaked. Kestrel realized she was not wearing her Towers disguise and her resemblance to her sister might have been shocking. "No, I'm Kestrel, Grace's sister."

Not knowing what else to do she stuck out her hand to him. He shook it, but it seemed he didn't realize what he was doing. Some color had come back into his face. "Oh, of course. Good to meet you."

The performer, on his arm, tugged gently. "Are you ready, Kev? I want to get changed and get something to eat."

"Sure." He looked at Kestrel and then turned and followed Sweetpea behind the curtain.

Kestrel returned to the table to find that Bobby had paid the bill and was waiting to leave. "What's up?"

"Nothing really, let's talk about it on the way home."

Once they were in the car Kestrel fell silent, thinking about what she had seen. "Bobby, I know it's private police business but did you guys talk to Grace's boyfriend, Kevin Durbin?"

"Yep, it didn't seem to me he was too broken up over Grace's death and his alibi wasn't bulletproof. But he doesn't seem to have been the guy."

"Where was he when Grace was killed?"

"He was here, I mean at Specs, that night. It was a Thursday, so about two hundred people saw him."

"I just saw him kissing one of the performers, Celine Dion, I think. Did he tell you that?"

"Not specifically, but it was kind of obvious when we interviewed Sweetpea, um, Jason. Why?"

"I don't know. Just, his grandmother was convinced he and Grace were going to get married. That just doesn't seem likely to me."

"Well, my grandmother keeps hoping I'll get married, too."

"Yeah, but yours isn't a millionaire and you don't go around groping drag queens. At least, not that I know of."

"His grandmother is probably in denial."

"I suppose." But Bobby hadn't seen the look on Kevin's face.

Suddenly Kestrel grabbed Bobby's arm causing the car to swerve. "Let's go back to the club, I need to ask Kevin a quick question."

"Kestrel, you need to stay out of this. It's police business and you are butting in again."

"It will just take a minute and then I will butt out."

"Kestrel..."

She'd heard that tone many times and didn't have time to get into an argument. "Okay, okay, take me back to my place."

When they got back to Kestrel's she hopped out of the car and hurried to open the door. Turning back toward him, she reached up to peck him on the cheek. "Well, it's been great, Bobby. We'll have to do it again sometime."

"Good night, then."

"Yep, good night." She quickly closed the door leaving him standing there. After a few moments he turned and went back to his car.

Kestrel turned off the porch light and stood just inside the door waiting for Bobby to pull his car away from the curb. Then she slipped back out the door, opened the garage, and fired up the VW. As she drove down the street she didn't notice Bobby's car pull out behind her about a block back. He hadn't known her this long without figuring out when he was being bamboozled.

The Castro district was quiet when Kestrel parked on the side street next to Specs. As she'd suspected there was a side door into the old building, and she grinned hugely when the handle turned and it swung inward. She could still hear the murmur of voices from the front of the house but she turned the other way toward what passed as dressing rooms. This area was cramped and ill-lit. Off the dim hallway, cubicles lined the wall, privacy shielded by heavy curtains. The first one was empty, but she nearly ran head-on into a young blond man when she pushed the second curtain aside.

"Oh, shit, you scared me." The slight young man laughed.

"Um, sorry. I was just looking for Sweetpea."

"That's me. Jason in street clothes, but Sweetpea in drag." He turned his head, looked over his shoulder and batted his eyelashes at her coyly. "What can I do for you? I'm just getting ready to leave. How did you get back here, anyway?"

He glanced past her toward the bar.

As Kestrel stepped toward him into the small dressing space, he backed up. The area contained a dressing table with mirror, a chair, and a clothes rack hung with bulky costume bags.

"You aren't supposed to be back here, you know. It ruins the illusion."

"I just want to ask you a couple of questions."

"Who are you, again? You're that girl that was talking to Kevin out there."

"Yes, my name is Kestrel and Grace Callahan was my sister."

At the mention of Grace's name, the already pale man blanched. "I don't know anything about her, I didn't even know her."

"But you knew of her, didn't you?"

"Of course I did. She was Kevin's cover-up. His beard, that kept his grandmother happy. She didn't mean anything to him, though."

"I believe you, Jason. But, did she know that, did she know about you?"

"No, I don't know. It doesn't matter what she knew." Jason's expression had become belligerent.

"No, it didn't matter what she knew." Kevin spoke right behind her. Kestrel jumped and let out a little shriek.

He stepped further into the space, which suddenly seemed very crowded with three of them in it. "She didn't know about you, either. One day she was an only child and the next day, voilà, she had siblings."

Kevin was smiling but Kestrel didn't feel very comforted.

Jason had picked up on the sense of menace as well and backed a little further toward the corner. "She came here to ask me questions about Grace. I told her I didn't know her or anything about her."

"No, you didn't. And, to answer her other question, Grace didn't know about you."

"But she found out, didn't she?" Kestrel guessed.

"Yeah, she found out, but I don't know how."

Jason piped up, "You thought I told her, but I didn't. I never talked to her."

"How the hell did she find out?" Kevin was really speaking to himself. Musing over the mystery.

"She found out because she saw you here. She came with some friends and she saw you here, together," Kestrel said.

"That would explain it." He laughed. "She was pissed off, but not about me being with Jason, because she felt I was fooling my grandmother, letting her think we were going to get married."

"Was she going to tell Lilah all about you?"

Suddenly alert, Kevin looked harder at her. "What do you know about Lilah? Who the hell are you, really?" He gripped her upper arm and pulled her face closer to him. "She got all high and mighty with me. Said I should come out to my family and stop trying to fool people just to get the money."

"Did that piss you off, Kevin?"

"I was mad, at first, then I figured I could talk her out of it if I was smart about it. She'd listen to me, she just felt sorry for Gram." Kev's face screwed up like he was about to cry, but morphed back into anger.

"Did you try to talk to Grace? Did you go back over to her place on Thursday?" Kestrel had slowly moved toward the curtain trying to sidle past Kevin.

A squeaking sob came from the corner that Jason had pulled further into and Kevin stepped toward him.

Kestrel took that moment to lunge toward the curtained exit but Kevin turned and grabbed her arm again.

"Come back here, you can't leave now." Kevin didn't look like he had a plan, but he did look determined to keep her there and shoved her in the direction of the clothes rack. "Just hold on a minute. I have to figure this out." Kevin stood still with both hands holding his head.

"It was just an accident. She was being a bitch, getting ready for her brother to bring some pictures. She didn't want to talk." Kevin dropped down into the lone chair and Jason moved to stand beside him, putting his arm across Kevin's shoulders as they began to shake. "I got pissed all over again but was going to leave and she shoved me. She shoved me backward toward the door and I shoved her back, hard. She stumbled back and fell. Her head hit the floor and knocked her out. I didn't check on her or anything, I just left her there. I didn't know she was dead but I kept waiting for her to report me to the police. I thought they'd arrest me."

"But when we came, it was to tell you that she was dead." Bobby stood at the curtained entrance.

"Yes…" Kevin had begun to sob and Jason patted his shoulder absently.

"You know, we might have thought it was an accident; that she fell, except for the missing phone and laptop."

Kevin started, "I didn't take her stuff."

"Yeah, we know who took it, too bad for both of you."

CHAPTER FORTY-SIX

Thanksgiving

Kestrel pulled to the curb in front of the nice home in Menlo Park and idled for a couple of minutes watching. The house was white with green shutters and surrounded by a slightly overgrown yard that displayed the last autumnal flowers. The late afternoon was already darkening and she could see lights shining from downstairs windows and the shadow of someone moving around in what she thought must be the dining room.

She eased the car forward to a space in front of the neighboring house to give herself a few minutes before she was noticed. As she turned off the ignition the VW coughed and sputtered a bit and finally died.

Since the finalization of the court settlement of Garrett Graham, Senior's trust she could easily have purchased a nicer car, but she hated to give up the little VW. She had to admit that, even with money in the bank, she was a used car and public-transit kind of gal.

On her drive down from San Francisco she had passed her Menlo Park exit and detoured through Palo Alto, driving past the place on Evergreen Court where her grandmother's home had stood. The suburban home built in the fifties had been razed and replaced with a McMansion that came as close to the property lines as possible and rose mightily to dwarf the trees in the yard. She'd driven past Castilleja, the private girls' school on Embarcadero that Grace had attended, and then past Palo Alto High School. She turned into Town and Country Shopping Center where she'd hoped to buy a pumpkin pie. Unfortunately, TJ's actually let their staff have Thanksgiving off. She'd been told she didn't need to bring anything but couldn't resist the urge to contribute to the meal. Isn't that what you did at family dinner? Not that she'd attended a lot of those types of gatherings.

If the old Stickney's had still been there she'd have bought a pie from them, or maybe a Coffee Crunch Cake, her early childhood favorite before Stickney's had gone the way of the dodo, so she settled for a pie from the Whole Foods on Emerson.

She'd had a couple of invites for Thanksgiving dinner but hoped this would give her an opportunity she was finally ready to face, the chance to get to know the couple who had raised Grace. It had been generous of them to invite her on this first holiday dinner since their daughter's death.

Next to her on the passenger seat were a bouquet of sunflowers, the pumpkin pie, a bottle of passable Prosecco, and the leather calendar journal that had belonged to Grace. She had brought the journal today to return it to its rightful owners.

The journal was her only personal link to her sister, and although it had helped solve the mystery of her murder and had given Kestrel some endearing glimpses into her sibling's mind, it didn't feel right to keep it. She'd found great comfort in the little book but thought it best belonged here in Grace's childhood home in the care of the couple who had raised her.

She'd even come up with a plausible excuse for having it. She would just tell them that Grace had loaned it to her on the one night they had spent together and she'd felt she needed to bring it back, which was almost the truth. Her mother, the consummate liar, could never remember the KISS (Keep It Simple, Stupid) theory of telling lies, thus her own prevarications were elaborate and confusing, usually ending in disaster.

It wasn't really a normal journal. It was a sort of mixture of observations, doodles, and impressions that Grace had used to help remember, and to wrap her head around what was happening in her life. The entry that Kestrel had taken a photo of was the one made the day after they first met. Doodled sunflowers and two stick figures in skirts running through the blooms, a bigger one and a smaller one. Written in a rambling cursive that squiggled between the girls and the flowers were the words, "Yesterday I found the missing piece of me that I always knew was there. It is a new beginning..."

Kestrel looked at that page one last time and ran her fingers over the curving text before she slipped the journal into her shoulder bag. Maybe she would return it today.

THE END

Made in United States
Orlando, FL
21 September 2022

22651475R00138